THIEF OF SPARKS

STARSIDE SAGA #1

ERIC KENT EDSTROM

To J

ATOP THE ROOFWAY

Every heart in Starside felt the soul-shivering flight of the raven. She swooped low over the Divide like smoke in shadow. Her onyx eyes glimmered, seeing all but seeking just one.

The night masked her flight, but every wakeful soul in Starside looked skyward. None knew why. It was an involuntary impulse, whether in bed or in a tavern or in the Citadel.

What was that? they asked in breathless whispers. Housemothers rubbed their elbows. Men scratched their chins and put on brave faces. Children cried out. The faithful offered timorous prayers. The faithless tipped back trembling cups. Dogs whimpered in their sleep.

The raven wheeled and beat back inland, searching, scanning, *feeling*. The one she sought was out in the city, while nobler hearts were in.

The one she sought was, like her, a scavenger.

Alas, she was also prey.

∾

UPON A CHANDLER's rooftop in Starside's lowest quarter, the barefoot thief wrinkled her nose and shivered. The odd feeling that had come over her just now slowly lifted from her shoulders. Strange. Kila Sigh had never been superstitious—and never fearful of the dark—but she looked behind her and questioned whether it might be better to return home than to stay out in this weird mist.

"My mind is just giving me the horrors," she whispered to herself. Father would have laughed to see her so shaky. This was the perfect time and place to ply her trade.

She summoned courage by muttering a curse, then turned her attention back to the street below. This *was* the perfect time and place. The damp cobblestones glimmered in the glare of the mercus lights. Her quarry would be easy to spot. The hour was late. The street was vacant.

She knew she had picked her mark well. A young man wandering home at the end of a long night of trezzing. Gauging by his fine cloak and boots, he was probably bound for a merchant's greathouse in Upper Terriside. Perfect. His purse would be heavy with coin.

She wrinkled her nose again, this time with impatience. Where was he? She'd trailed him from Critt Sanglo's tavern in Cheaspgate. He'd been staggering so badly it had been nothing to race atop the roofway to get ahead of him. He'd be easy.

The Street of Sorrows was well lit by the bluish

white mercus lights that made late night wanderers feel safe. It was quite the opposite. Bright lights make deep shadows. He would never spot her up here on the rooftop.

Fine rain needled down now. Kila huddled in her sodden shirt and trousers, flexing her bare feet against the cedar shingles to keep them warm. The chill was becoming dangerous now. "Kil's eyes in a bucket, where is he?" He simply could not pass this spot without her seeing him

A door closed somewhere down the street. She levered herself out over drop to see. Nothing. Probably a shop maid dumping her mop bucket into the gutter. A dog barked in the distance and was answered from one nearer by. Whatever the hounds said to each other must not have been too interesting, for both went silent after a brief exchange.

Kila liked dogs. Once she'd saved enough coin, she and her brother were going to stop thieving. They'd get a little shop over on Sidle Street with an apartment up top. Then they'd get a dog to stand guard at night. Maybe two.

The thin tune of a drunk man's song lifted to her ears.

She crouched and rocked side to side, trying to get warmth back into her legs. Her hand absently patted her thigh. Cayne wasn't there. Wen never let her bring their father's blade when she was out robbing. The Watch released pickpockets after a night in the Westbunk. But if they caught you armed, they'd take the blade and a hand.

Her mark staggered up the Street of Sorrows, singing "She Stoops to Kiss Him." It was one of Kila's favorites, an old bawdy about a tall girl who loved a short boy. The later verses were confusing, though, and Wen would never tell her what they meant. Just that the girl was improbably flexible.

The man came into view. He had a sack slung over his shoulder. It looked like a stretch of sailcloth bound and tied at one end. Something lumpy inside. Maybe some old socks, or few cabbages. But she refused to believe it. This time of night, him leaving a tavern, she was sure his makeshift sack held gambling winnings. The mere idea of it warmed her guts.

She wished Wen was with her. She could imagine him crouched alongside her, eyes alight with excitement. Nobody loved stalking a mark more than he did. But he was back in their den, trying not to cough up his lungs. Kila pushed the thought away. One problem at a time. Rob this drunkard first; buy Wen's medicine with the takings. *"Put on your pants before your shoes,"* Father had always said.

She watched the man pass below her, gauging his size and strength. He didn't look too bulky. Hard to really know, covered as he was in that heavy cloak. The buckles on his boots jingled with every step. Face shrouded deep in his hood. She guessed he was about eighteen.

There was too much light in this area for her to roll him here. She'd follow him until he turned off the Sorrows. That he hadn't turned off already meant he was heading for Upper Terriside. The wealthiest merchants lived there.

But what if he wasn't a merchant? If he continued through the Harridan Gate . . . That would make him the son of a Radiant. She was dying to know how much coin he carried.

There was a way to find out before ever laying hands on him.

She closed her eyes and felt for it, the buzzy sensation that came before her vision sharpened and the *thing* happened. The thing. The disconcerting, terrifying, exhilarating *thing*. The talent she'd been blessed with, but which she couldn't invoke at will. The buried, unnatural, ability that showed her the world in its infinite detail. The overwhelming rush of sensation that took over and revealed the unseeable. She loved it, she hated it, she feared it.

"Never ever speak of it," Father had told her. *"They'll take you from us."* And the way he'd said it, the fierce defiance in his eyes, the clenching of his fist, told her that he would die to prevent that. Alas, he had died saving someone else.

The thing did not happen. Her secret skill remained secret even to her.

The drunk man passed. She stood and groaned at the stiffness in her knees. She bounced on her toes and swung her arms to limber up. Her favorite part of the job was about to begin.

The run.

She backed from the ledge and paced off ten spans. She needed to get her speed up for the first jump. And then she was off, sprinting. Her bare feet tapped the shingles, muscles collecting power, and then she was soaring across the lane. Instinct guided her feet to find the opposite rooftop. She dropped and rolled to take up some of the momentum, then popped to her feet.

The roofway was known to the shopowners, of course. Few nights passed without some thief or other making noise over their heads. But there was a system, an agreement, sorted out long ago between shop-keepers and thieves. Thieves paid tolls and agreed not to rob the shops. In return, thieves could use the roofway to quickly traverse the city.

Kila dropped a copper plug into a toll pail. A boy would come up in the morning to collect it. Occasion-ally someone would abuse the roofway and a few merchants would hire a man to enforce the rules. Word got around fast when a thief was found on a roof with a flickbow bolt in his neck.

She raced toward the stone wall of Lac Wagner's hack house. Her toes planted on the vertical face. Here —then here—then here, she thrusted up until her fingers found the ledge. Her shoulders burned as she pulled, launching herself well above the lip of the roof. She landed in stride,

The tolls weren't just for safe passage.

Her heart slammed with the thrill to come. A long jump. A quiet grunt and she was airborne again. Her legs wheeled as she flew across the gap. The street passed far below. This was as close to flying as a girl could get. It didn't last long. She was falling now, wind whipping her hair back in a long stream. The roof of the Yin Inn approached, faster and faster.

A burlap mat the size of an ox absorbed her impact. It was stuffed fat and tight with straw. She dropped into a roll, then popped to her feet. The toll pails paid for the mats, too. Somebody had to keep them stuffed and properly placed. Kila would use three more before her run was done. Her copper plinked into the pail and she was gone.

Another jump. A kick of wind shoved her sideways. Not enough to trouble her. She landed and skidded to a stop. Nostrils flaring with huge inhalations, she bent double to collect herself. Steam lifted from her arms. A storm was rolling in from the sea somewhere behind her. She caught a whiff of salt air and rotting fish. It smelled like home.

She inched to the edge of the roof to check on her mark's progress. The Street of Sorrows lay below her. It was a bit wider here, the paving stones better maintained. This was Upper Terriside. Her quarry came around the bend just when she anticipated. Soon he'd turn off on one of the nearby side streets. Or he'd continue to the Harridan Gate. In either case, she was in the perfect position.

Someone emerged from an alley behind her mark, vague and shadowy. He was gone in an instant, but she'd noted the distinct posture of someone sneaking.

A thief.

Someone else stalking *her* mark. A growl vibrated in her throat. That purse was hers. That sack was hers.

The drunk man passed her spot, song fading as he

continued his stumbling trek home. She waited to see what his pursuer did. It didn't take long. The villain emerged from a door niche and hustled along, hugging the buildings on her side of the street. His skills might have worked in shadows, but not in the full glare of the mercus streetlights. What an idiot.

There was no excuse for trailing mark on street level. What sort of thief would do that? A stupid one. He'd been lucky to come this far undetected, but Pol—goddess of luck—wasn't smiling on him now. Kila was going to make the take before he had a chance to scare the man and make him wary.

She gathered her focus and ran. Over Glinny Lane, around the courtyard of the tax house. Full speed for the long leap over Smithwest Street. Into the air. Knees absorbing the landing. Shuffling along a ledge to a downspout.

Climb up, sprint.

Jump!

Hold breath . . .

Hard landing on the stuffed mat over Harlinton Tailors. Copper in the pail, not breaking stride. Another leap, arms outstretched. She caught a thick metal flagpole jutting from the front of the Myton Theater. She let her momentum carry her in a circle, then shot feet-first to an overhang overlooking the street.

She went very still. Her mark was twenty paces ahead. No sign of the other thief. Her breath heaved in her chest and her limbs were warm and alive. Every object in the world was crisp, despite the mist. Even the sounds came to her with more clarity. If a gull squawked a mile away, she'd hear.

Ah. This was it. The buzzing in her limbs, the keen senses. She decided to try the thing again. She relaxed and let her eyes go passive. The sensation built all around her, like standing at the center of a storm, in a tiny circle of calm. She waited, strained, and then caught herself grasping for it. Too late. She lost it, and again the world became mundane.

No matter, that nuisance thief had just emerged from the alley below her. He must have run flat out to come so far so fast. Her route over the roofways was half the distance he must have traveled. He was winded, breath pluming into the chill air. A very young man. She revised his age down a year. Maybe two. In any case, not much older than she was. His clothes were shabby but better than her homemade rags. The lad was thin, no doubt about that. His hair was black, chopped short. She didn't recognize him.

So much for her plan to rob her mark before this fool got close enough to scare him off. There was nothing for it but to discourage him directly. Shouldn't take long. If he was this inexperienced at stalking, he was probably scared half to death already.

She pulled her hair back from her face and knotted it atop her head. She'd learned not to give her enemies hair to grab. She blew a stray lock out of her eye and waited. Once the thief had slunk farther down the street, she dropped to the paving stones behind him. She crept along, hand absently searching for Cayne. Not there, of course.

The thief stopped at a cross street and ducked into a little alcove. At least he was smart enough to stay out of the light when he had the chance. Not that her quarry would have noticed. The man's song carried down the street. If he didn't clam up, people would wake up and start shouting. Then there would be dozens of eyes on the street. Kila did not want that, especially after Wen's warning earlier than night. Before she'd left their den he'd grabbed her sleeve. "May Pol smile on you, sister. And remember, no witnesses."

Kil's teeth, did he ever know how to burn her biscuits. No witnesses! What did he think she was? A starving pickpocket going after her first purse?

The drunkard's song was fading. She had to get to him before he turned off or went through the Harridan Gate. Too many Watch patrols beyond the gate.

But first, her competition.

She waited for the lousy thief to emerge from the alcove, her body tense and relaxed at the same time. Just as Father had taught her.

The boy darted across the street. He headed for a doorway alcove further along. Kila would have made the same dash if she were stupid enough to trail a mark on street level.

She sprinted after him. He didn't hear her. Inexperienced thieves tended to become so focussed on their target they blocked out everything else. She jumped him, wrapping her arms around his neck, jamming a leg in front of both of his. They went down together; his body broke her fall.

His breath burst out in a pained gasp. "Kil's eyes! Ow!"

He wriggled to get free of her. She let him roll onto his back, but she wasn't done. Her fist jammed into the divot at the base of his throat while her legs pinned his. He struggled like a landed blubfish until she jammed her fist in harder. That always ended a struggle quickly.

The boy was lean, just skin and bones. And ugly! His face looked like a mummer's mask of Kil.

"That's *my* mark yer followin', lad," she said, making her voice raspy and low.

"You're—you're that girl Kila Sigh!" His voice came out a duck's quack from the pressure on his throat.

"An' here I thought you were stupid," she said. Nostrils flaring, she punched his gut. She dismounted as he grimaced and folded. That would do him for now.

"I'll forgive ya stalkin' my mark this time," she said. "But never again after this night. I see ya in this section of Terriside, I'll—" An impact from behind took her down, cheek grinding into the wet pavers. Weight crushed her and a dagger flashed in front of her eyes.

"Get up, Fallo!" said the boy on top of her.

Fallo was getting to his knees. With his thatch of black hair and a hideous face, he looked like a scream-clown ready to suck the soul of a newborn babe. "Jab her, Hen!"

Kila's attacker hesitated.

And he hadn't trapped her legs.

A dagger could make up for many deficiencies in a brawl, but this boy's incompetence was insulting. You always, always, always immobilize your opponent's legs.

She kicked a foot to the side, using the momentum to roll. The boy yelped and fell off. She gripped his wrist, jamming her thumb into his tendons until she found the sweet spot. He hissed; the weapon clanked onto the stones. Her knee drove into his groin, and that was that.

She sprang up, snatching the dagger.

Fallo had gotten to his feet, but he was holding his belly and trying to catch his breath. The other boy had folded into a ball, keening.

Kila twirled the dagger. "I won't warn you boys again."

She ran down the street, racing to catch up to her drunken mark. A minute later she was on the roofway. Something pulled in her mind, a nagging thought. She realized what it was. Wen's admonishment about witnesses. But surely those boys didn't count.

It didn't matter. She needed that purse. She would have it, and the sack.

THE AWAKENING MERCULYN

Dunne Skyll left the crypt, taking great caution to close the door softly. One did not make unnecessary noise near the Hargothe. Once into the dim corridor, he let his shoulders sag as he blew out a long breath. No matter how many times he was in the great seer's presence, he never grew accustomed to the heavy quietude of the room, nor the man's cruelty.

What Skyll needed was a cup of trezz and an hour in open air. As a Donse Master of Til, he wasn't supposed to indulge in hard spirits. But was a little swallow truly an indulgence? It didn't matter. The Hargothe had sifted through his thoughts, knew all his sins. Well, maybe not *all* of them. There were a few that the Hargothe would never forgive. And if he'd discovered them, Skyll would already be dead.

Mopping his forehead with a kerchief, Dunne Skyll began his trek up from of the deep levels of the Abbey of Til. By the time he emerged into the Cathedral, his whole body was sticky and prickly with sweat. His robes clung to his body. This made him irritable and he snapped at an acolyte who approached him with a summons from Highest Chilow. Skyll had served two masters for a decade, and he had navigated those straits deftly. But his instructions from the Hargothe were clear. Find the awakening merculyn and bring him in.

Highest Chilow might be head of the Way of Til, but the Hargothe was the true power here. Skyll would obey him first. Chilow would understand, for even he did not dare to contradict the sickly seer.

"Gather the senior cohort and meet me in the plaza," he said to the acolyte, a twenty year old man with gaunt eyes and bulging throat apple. "We must apprehend a baby merculyn."

"Yes, Dunne Skyll. Shall I fetch some armsmen?"

This gave Skyll pause, for it was a political question as much as it was a practical one. The Way of Til did not have armsmen in its direct employ. Instead the Way relied on a volunteer regiment, supplied by wealthy patrons. Whenever the Way deployed them, the city Watch complained. But the Hargothe's demands were clear. A squad of armed and armored men would give Skyll more obvious authority and discourage the merculyn from fleeing.

"Eight men, Acolyte Muin. Hurry. The Hargothe says the merculyn is out in the city even now."

The acolyte hustled away and Dunne Skyll ventured outside to Dunne Medow Plaza. He cursed the rain and pulled his hood up. His old bones hated autumn in Starside. It was too damp and cold. He slipped his mercus relic from its sleeve on his belt. A short ivory rod, warm in his hand. The Stonebone heller, fashioned an age ago by the First Race. No one knew how it had been made, but Skyll knew how to use it.

He went to the fountain in the center of the plaza and sat on the ledge. Closing his eyes, he fell into the customary meditation of a Seeker. His skill in feeling out merculyns was nothing compared to the Hargothe's, but if he got close enough he would feel him.

He'd barely counted ten breaths when he felt the surge upon the mercusine. He clutched his chest. Such power! And so close by.

No wonder the Hargothe wanted this merculyn. He would be a danger to himself and to the city. But where was he? Skyll closed his eyes and again sank into the mercusine web, the illuminated realm that pervaded the world. But the merculyn had vanished. Not surprising, those on the verge always wobbled in and out.

The clank and clatter of approaching armsmen drew him out of his meditation. He scowled at them until they went silent. "Wait. I must Seek." He closed his eyes.

STREET OF SORROWS

Fighting with those silly boys had taken too much time. Now Kila had to race to get ahead of her mark. Her frantic course over the rooftops filled her limbs with buzzing energy. It was pure aliveness, and she loved it. Her irritation with the boys faded as she ran. Her irritation with herself was slower to recede.

There had been two of them. One had kept to the shadows and alleys, while the other had trailed the mark on the street. She should have expected that. After all, she wouldn't be alone if Wen weren't sick.

She needed to stop thinking about those scoundrels. There was a job to do. She came to a stop on the first floor overhang of a boarding house right where the Street of Sorrows ended at the Harridan Gate. The street narrowed here and made a slight jog to the right where it entered the long, low tunnel. The so-called gate wasn't blocked by any doors or portcullises. The name had come down through the centuries following an uprising against Queen Duri. The rebellous citizenry had thrown up a barricade in this spot to keep the queen's forces from coming into Terriside. Those who despised her had circulated leaflets calling Duri "The Harridan Queen." The barrier was swiftly demolished, but the people continued to call the passage by its new name. The Harridan Gate. Today it was a long arch-roofed carriageway where two buildings connected over the street. The resulting tunnel was dank, smelling always of stale wine and urine. Nobody liked going through it, but it was the only way to Gristenside.

Satisfied that she was hidden in deep shadow, Kila knelt on the overhang. She was soaked to the skin, and the night was growing colder. She needed to roll this fellow and get back to the den and out of these wet clothes. No sign of her mark, though, and not a hint of song in the air. Maybe he'd worn out his throat. Maybe he was too winded to continue singing. Starside was a steep city, built in tiers ascending from the docks. From Cheapsgate to Gristenside was a five mile journey, uphill.

The bell of the Cathedral of Til let out a single sonorous gong. Kila leaned out to looked down the street. Had she missed him? She didn't see how that would be possible along this stretch of the Sorrows. It was mostly tidy, shoulder-to-shoulder shops. A couple of turrets thrust up from the larger inns.

Impatience tempted her to drop to the street and backtrack to see if he'd passed out. She cut off that impulse. Her sprint along the roofway had filled her with so much energy, she wasn't sensing the passage of time accurately. A lesson learned long ago. She took hold of a bit of decorative filigree on the boarding house wall so she could lean further out. The drop was enough to break her legs, but she wasn't afraid of heights. In fact, she loved being up high, especially when she knew she couldn't be seen.

Her foot slipped an inch, her breath caught. She pulled back from the ledge, heart skipping. She hadn't been in true danger of falling, but her body didn't know that. The buzzing aliveness rushed up to sizzle in her ears.

And then it happened. The thing.

After all that straining and grasping, suddenly it happened by itself.

The mercus vision came over her.

First came the dizziness, and the doubling of all she could see. The noise of raindrops striking the shingles and the paving stones increased to a loud hiss. Then other sounds came to her. Of runoff gurgling through gutters and downspouts, of the breeze bending over rooftops, of buildings creaking and settling all around her. Then came the smells. The fishy odor of Cheapsgate, blending with chimney smoke and the tang of the tanneries. This all mixed with the smell of wet paving stones and the sweat of her own skin.

She knelt and supported herself with her hands. She knew what was coming next. It always overwhelmed her as much as it thrilled her.

The doubled vision resolved to perfect, crisp unity.

The sounds and smells remained, but each became distinct.

And then the metal around her began to glow.

First came the reddish aura of copper rain gutters on the building across the way. Then came the ruddier, grimier light of iron grates covering the sewer drains in the street. Then the brass door latches at shop entries.

Objects that weren't in her line of sight popped into view. The great bell atop of the Cathedral of Til hovered like an occluded sun off to her right. So too did the brass lanterns and pewter candlesticks in the boarding house behind her. She took all this in, frozen still. She witnessed it all through the mind of a babe, innocent to language itself. Sensation washed over her, filling her nose and eyes and ears with sparkling wonder.

The mercus vision had come to her only three times before. Each time it had followed a moment of danger, a moment when the buzzing in her bones exploded into her mind.

Her quarry's footsteps were crisp and distinct to her now. She heard him grunt as he shifted his burden on his shoulder. Heard him sigh and belch softly. And then he appeared, moving much more slowly than before. His hood was pushed back. His hair was white in the mercus streetlights. His skin porcelain. He was one of the Keel brothers. Not a Radiant's son. So why was he coming this way? The Keel greathouse was a half mile south. He should have turned off onto Harbor Prospect.

No time to speculate. He was right beneath her.

He stopped and set down his sack. With hurried motions he unfastened his trousers. The sound urine striking the wall crackled in her ears. Instinct guided her now. She dropped from the overhang, catching her hands on the ledge. She hung there for a moment then released, falling the last distance in a belly lifting plummet.

Feet struck stone, knees bending deep to absorb the impact. And then she was up, approaching her mark with confident steps. He was struggling to fasten up his trousers. He fumbled with a buckle. It glowed a bright silver in her mercus vision. The buttons on his waistcoat were brass. He carried a small knife on his belt. No sign of coin, which was odd for one of his station.

She kicked the back of his right knee. It folded, he fell back, flailing. She caught him under the arms, turned him and thrust him face down into the paving stones. He was much heavier than she, but surprise gave her the edge. She drove her knee into his spine, then pressed her stolen dagger to the nape of his neck. "Hold still."

He froze.

Her finger found the button holding his purse onto his belt. A practiced twist and pull brought it free. Fine leather, but shamefully empty.

"Where's your coin, Keel?" she raspsed into his ear.

"I—I don't have any."

Just her luck. A son of the richest merchant in the

city and his purse was busted. "Forgot where you live, Keel?" she asked.

"What?"

"Why you going to Gristenside? Think you can get a Radiant's daughter to marry you?"

"A Radiant's what? Are you a *girl*?"

She put more weight on his spine. "What's in the sack?"

"Nothing! Some old boots I was going to donate to the Abbey."

At one bell morning? That was a lie. She glanced at the sack and then at the back of his head. His hair was like pewter now that it was wet. She pressed the point of the dagger to the skin behind his ear. "Move and I'll cut it off," she said, slowly removing her knee from his back.

"I won't move. I won't!"

But she was already off him. She grabbed the sack and sprinted away. The young man's yells arose behind her, incredibly loud to her mercus-hieghtened senses. "THIEF! HELP! MURDER!"

Kila squeezed the sack tightly to her chest as she sprinted a block east, going downhill, then darted down an alley to a well known roof-climb behind a guild hall. Whatever was inside the bag, it was moving. An animal. Kila sniffed at it. A pungent, wild odor came through the sailcloth. The wriggling wasn't too vigorous. Whatever it was, it had probably been in the sack a while. "Kil's eyes! I better not have wasted my night for a Cheapsgate chicken." Which was the polite name for seagull.

Once safely hidden upon the roofway, she unfastened the tie and peered into the sack. There wasn't any light here, so she couldn't make out much. But a pair of green eyes looked back at her. She dropped the sack and backpedaled. "Kil's teeth! A demayne."

The sack wobbled a moment, then a small gray head popped out. The eerie eyes fixed on her a moment, then the whole beast appeared. Her instant fear gave way to confusion. She didn't know what the creature was. Despite its bedraggled state, the animal was well proportioned. Standing on four legs, it recalled to mind a tiny dog. In the darkness it was hard to make out much else.

She knelt and tilted her head. "Are you good to eat?" she asked it. All this running had doubled her hunger. She wasn't much more than ribs herself. The animal blinked at her. It didn't seem afraid. In fact, it seemed mostly disgruntled. Its tail swished in sharp jerks. It had white feet and a streak of white from chin down the chest. It stepped toward her, tentative now. And no wonder. Kila wouldn't forgive being stuffed in a sack either.

Her eyelids grew heavy. She dropped from her crouch to sitting, insensible to the wetness seeping through the seat of her pants. The cold was closing in on her again.

The animal came to within arm's reach. She snatched for it. The animal leapt straight up in the air, twisted mid-flight, and sprang away. Kila scurried after it, but it was gone. She looked in the sack, disconsolate. "Kil be a merry maiden. What a crummy night."

Now she had to go back to the den empty-handed. Not even a silver skillet to warm her palm. She didn't have enough copper plugs to pay the toll pails along the way. Which meant she had to go against her honor and stiff them, or she had to go on the street.

She scooped up the sack, thinking that at least she could show Wen she'd stolen something. He'd laugh at her. But he wouldn't blame her. He'd say something kind, like, "You tried your best. Sometimes Pol frowns, no matter how skilled we are."

The goddess of luck could go kiss a slubfish, for all Kila cared. The mercus vision had vanished now, and she was glad of it. The long trek home was going to be bad enough as it was, she didn't need to hear every raindrop as it needled into her face.

She climbed down from the roof and headed east, taking the switchbacks of the Street of Sorrows. The sound of boots behind spun her around. At first she thought it was the Watch answering the Keel boy's cries. And indeed, a squad of armsmen was tromping downhill toward her. But they were behind a band of ten men in tan robes.

Acolytes of Til. The worst. Anyone associated with the Way of Til was not to be trusted. And there was a Donse Master with them.

"You there! Halt!" shouted one of the armsmen.

She slipped into a little shoulder-width alley between a cobbler's shop and a dry goods store. At the end she cut left, skittering down some rather slick stairs. There was no light here. Her hand glided over the old wood handrail. She didn't need light; her feet knew the way.

One of the acolytes knew it just as well. He called out for his friends to race to Old Turret, which was right were Kila was going to come out. She flung the sack behind her and sprinted as hard as she could.

And then her legs went rigid. Her heels juddered on the pavement. Her momentum carried her forward, arms locked mid pump. She struck shoulder first, slid and cartwheeled like a tossed plank. She flopped onto her spine.

She couldn't move.

Panic took control. Breath heaved in and out. She strained to move her limbs, but they were frozen in place. Footsteps approached. Heavy boots splashed puddles into her face and thick hands took hold of her. She wanted to curse them, wanted to scream. Her mouth wouldn't move. Not even her tongue.

"Bring her into the light, men," came a quiet masculine voice. It was stained with age. Had she been free to struggle, even four of these powerful armsmen would have had a job of hauling her along. But now a single man carried her as easily and calmly as he might shoulder a cask of beer out of a cellar.

The mercus streetlight pierced her eyes as they came out onto the Sorrows.

"Put her down."

The wet street thumped against her back. She could only move her eyes. The Donse Master stood right at the edge of her vision. He held a slender little rod in one hand. It seemed to glow a bit, or maybe that was just the mercus light blooming in the mist.

"Stand back, armsmen," he ordered. "I must consult with my acolytes."

Soon she was surrounded by young men in tan robes. And at her head, bending to peer down at her, the Donse Master. She wanted to kick his white-bearded chin. Wanted to grab his long gray locks and pull them out of his scalp. He was using the mercus on her!

"I think it's a girl," he said, pursing his lips.

"Want me to check?" said one of the acolytes. This produced a few laughs, but they cut off at a stern look from the Donse Master. He squatted and gently curled a sodden lock from Kila's brow. He smelled faintly of pipe smoke. He had wiry nose hairs.

His hand was warm and dry as he pressed it to her forehead. Kila's muscles were contracted still in her running posture, one arm slightly back, one slightly forward. Her right leg was bent up, locked mid-stride. As much as she wanted to lash out, she also couldn't relax a single fiber.

"It's her," the Donse Master said, finally opening his eyes. His tone suggested disbelief. "The Seer will be delighted." He stood, knees popping. He let out a soft groan. "Armsmen, do any of you have bindings? I must release her from the relic soon or she'll be irreversibly damaged."

Clanks and jingles of armor approached. An armsman pulled a bundle of thin leather cords from a pouch. He knelt and took hold of Kila's raised wrist.

He tried to twist her arm behind her back, but the Donse Master's mercus relic kept her rigid as a statue. Her skin burned as he tried to force her arm.

"Hold a moment," the Donse Master said. "I'll release her." He looked at his little rod and gave it a flick. Kila's muscles released. And with it, so was her fury. The armsman wasn't ready for it. She wriggled like a snake on fire. Her knuckles smashed his nose. He grunted and released her.

Her rabid snarls drove the acoloytes back, hiking the hems of their robes. The Donse Master fumbled to retrieve his rod from his belt. She scrabbled onto all fours and charged him, wrapping her arms around his knees. Grunting, she lifted him off his heels and drove his spine to the ground. His head gave a terrific crack. Kila didn't pause to see if his eyes rolled up or if his scalp bloomed with blood. She was already sprinting back into the alley, up the stairs, past the discarded sack.

The cries of armsmen and acolytes grew hollow in the narrow passage behind her. The breadth of the Sorrows was a brief flash of brightness as she raced to the safety of a shadowed sidestreet. She pounded down the lane, scaled a fence, and dropped into somebody's garden. She trampled late autumn kale and squash, then hurdled the front gate. No shouts or signs of pursuit now, but she did not pause. Climbing to the roofway, she leaped and sprinted toward Lower Terriside. Going downslope, the roofs were successively lower, making the journey all the swifter. She vowed to come back later and pay the tolls once she had any copper to part with. For now she accepted the debts out of neccessity.

The city's ring wall came closer and she deemed it was safe to slow down. There was no way those Tilsboys and armsmen knew where she was now. She considered stopping and trying to use her mercus vision. Maybe she could spot the glow of their armor and swords from afar. She decided against it. She was too wet, too cold, and too scared to stay out.

Her cheek burned where it had scraped along the alley pavement. Her quilted shirt was black with greasy mud. It clung to her skin like paint. She angrily wiped tears away. She made her way to the sewer grate behind the Cherry Bottom Inn. She wouldn't dare to pass through the Cheaps now. The safest route was a bit longer, but she'd take it. Through the sewers, under the wall, and into the slums of Cheaspgate. With any luck, she'd be home before the bells struck two.

4
———

SOCKETS WERE EMPTY

The back of Dunne Skyll's head felt like it had been bludgeoned with a ten-weight sledge. His shoulders wouldn't relax an inch, and merely turning his head sent jagged jolts down his spine. He would never have though a scrawny girl of sixteen could be strong enough to lift him from his feet.

Despite his injury, he bade the acolytes and armsmen to give chase. He waited on the Sorrows until the bells tolled three. The acolytes had already reuturned by then, not as shamefaced as they ought to have been. The armsmen were still out searching, but not as energetically as the should. Only their captain's pride kept them hunting. Dunne Skyll knew it was a waste of effort. The girl was like a rat. She would squeeze into a hole and hide.

Back in his quarters at the Abbey, Skyll submitted to the attentions of Dunne Yples, the most powerful healer in the Way of Til. But despite the man's skill, the gash on the back of Skyll's head continued to seep. Yples was vain and pious, two of the most annoying qualities in a religious man. He insisted in hearing about what had happened, but Skyll spoke only in vague terms about an awakening merculyn girl. The details were for the Hargothe's ears alone.

"It might be best to send word to Voluptuary Sinlop at the Baths of Ori," Dunne Ylpes said. "Even should you apprehend this girl, she obviously cannot come here." The Way of Til was the domain of men. Women who awakened to the mercus were foisted onto the lesser sisterhoods of the goddesses Ori and Pol. As a Seeker, Dunne Skyll knew that women were sometimes just as powerful in the mercus as any man.

The Hargothe did not mean to make Sigh an acoloyte. She was to be his possession, a source of mercus power he would tap to sustain himself. Dunne Skyll hated the man for such abuses, but he feared him more.

And now Skyll would have to go into the man's crypt and tell him the girl had gotten away. It might have been better for Skyll if he'd never awakened. Rubbing his head, he thanked Dunne Yples and pretended to sleep. Once the man was gone, he pulled on his robes and took up a walking stick to keep himself upright. The trek down into the cellars beneath the Cathedral took what little remaining strength he had. By the time he had reached the Hargothe's door, he was tempted to lie down in the corridor and sleep.

But there were always acolytes standing by to

serve the Hargothe. They were men of little mercusine power and enormous loyalty. They wore soft-soled shoes and special robes that made little noise. The Hargothe detested noise. An elderly acolyte guided Skyll into the silent room.

A mercus light glowed very dimly on one wall. The low, arched ceiling forced Dunne Skyll to duck as he entered. He was careful to step over the channels carved into the floor where steaming water ran in a continuous circuit. This was to heat the air, for the Hargothe was sickly and could not abide the cold.

If one did not know to look closely, one might think the bed unoccupied. The Hargothe was frail. Surpassing frail. He was a skeleton with skin. His face a skull, stretched with pale flesh and deep eyesockets. Wisps of gray hair stood out from a spotted scalp.

The eyes opened, but no eyeballs caught the glow of the mercus light. The sockets were empty.

Pale, cracked lips drew back from yellow teeth. "You failed," the Hargothe rasped.

Dunne Skyll considering shifting blame to the armsman who had underestimated Sigh's ferocity. But the Hargothe would not accept that. So Skyll merely nodded and whispered an apology. One never raised one's voice above a whisper here. To a Seeker of modest ability, which described Skyll perfectly, the Hargothe's mercus potential blazed like the sun. Dunne Yples potential had been a vauge haze by comparison.

Nobody knew how the Hargothe had come into his powers, though rumors spoke of blood rituals conducted in the southern islands of Ititti. But as any merculyn knew, such power came with a heightened sensitivity to all five senses. This deep crypt was designed to protect the Hargothe from the agonies of this supreme sensitivity.

"Tell me of her," the Hargothe said. His voice came in croaking bursts.

How to answer? Skyll knew this interview would not end with him speaking. It would end with him on his knees and the Hargothe probing around in his mind. There was nothing he could say that would prevent it. But the Hargothe always made him speak first. It was a test. For when he rifled through Skyll's thoughts later, he would uncover any ommissions or lies.

Skyll reported the encounter as best he could remember, leaving nothing out. He ended with an impression of Sigh's power. "Her mercus flickers. It's like lightning, blinding in flashes, then gone."

"I feel that too," the Hargothe said. "She is peculiar. Odd for a female to be so powerful. I don't like it. I must have her. I must. You are weak, Dunne Skyll. Do you meditate at all upon the mercusine web?"

"Daily, Seer Hargothe."

"You are nearly as blind to the mercus as I am to sight. I feel all merculyns. The whores at the Baths of Ori, the harlots in Pol's Well. That hateful witch in the Citadel. They all spark in my awareness, taunting me. I take comfort knowing that all will soon bow to me, palms up, to offer their mercus for my use. To glorify Til and serve his will. The world is a foul, corrupt wasteland. But the the visions I have seen! Ah, Dunne Skyll, if you only knew what glory is to come." The boney hand lifted from beneath a sheer blanket and reached for him.

Skyll knew what to do. But it was hard to simply resign oneself to pain. Harder still to put aside the fear that the Hargothe would discover his most closely held secret. Nothing he could do could prevent it. Only the Hargothe's disinterest in his personal life had spared him—and others—thus far.

The bony hand beckoned. The pain in Skyll's neck and back nearly tore cries from from his throat as he struggled to his knees. But to release such yelps would surely be the death of him. He put his head where the Hargothe could lay his cold, dry claw on it. The mind probe thrust in with no delicacy, no courtesty. It was a spike into his thoughts. The pain of his head wound had been appalling; this intrusion multiplied it. The violation began.

It lasted an eternity, and Dunne Skyll was sensible to his own release only when his cheek struck the floor. He was helped to his feet and guided from the presence of the Hargothe. Already the Seer's new instructions were compelling him to climb out of the cellars. No conversation had been needed when the Hargothe was able to simply plant his wishes into Skyll's mind.

He went to his own room and changed his clothes, ate a quick breakfast, and drew up a list. He handed this last to an acolyte and went to see Highest Chilow. Their conversation was brief and full of cursing. But there was nothing Chilow could do to stop events from proceeding as the Hargothe had directed. Everyone knew that the old seer was the true power behind the Way of Til in Starside.

And now he was going to come out of his crypt for the first time in twelve years.

5

NO WITNESSES

The ancient elnisian-built quays had long ago been overbuilt with warehouses, a press of wind-rattled structures frosted with sea salt and half-rotted from the damp.

But as the slums of Cheapsgate had spread, a different sort of rot had taken over. This one pocking not only timbers, but human souls. The incoming cargo ships no longer trusted their wares to the old buildings, and new ones inside the city walls took over. The old ones were abandoned, and soon claimed by the indigent masses who slept outside the city walls.

The Warren was the largest of these, home to two hundred wretched souls. Kila and Wen rented a little compartment at the end of a slanted passage on its second floor. Every wall inside the place was made wood pulled from wrecked ships, old crates, and other bits of scrap scavenged from the beaches.

Kila returned to the den through loose planks she and Wen had so cleverly fashioned. A secret doorway. To get to it required her to traverse the well-patched roof and descend the outside wall pon a crude ladder made from nailed-on scrapwood. It required a brief dangle over the Sourwater Inlet, a water befouled by the city's sewers. To fall into the Sourwater was to to die. She'd known one fellow—Tone Grilo—who had been thrown in my drunken friends. He suffered for a ten-day and died with bloody blisters on his neck, armpits, and groin.

She slipped into the den and fitted the planks snugly back in place. Darkness enfolded her. Wen's breathing told her he was asleep. She stripped off her sodden rags and blotted her skin dry with her blanket. Neither of them had a stitch of clothing extra, so she lay on her pallet of scraps and huddled under her blanket. Shivering, she hoped Lumne would claim her soon and spare her any dreams at all.

It was not to be. Wen spoke. "Kila?"

His voice was thin. He muffled a phlegmy cough and called to her again. "How did it go?"

Again she was glad of the darkness. She didn't want him to see her face. She couldn't bear to see his either, to see both his compassion and his illness. "I rolled a mark heading to Gristenside. I thought he was a Radiant's son, but he turned out to be a Keel. I trailed him all the way from Critt Sanglo's tavern to the Harridan. His purse was empty."

"Probably lost it gambling. Or drinking. Which Keel?"

"I don't know. They all look the same with their snowy hair."

In the silence that followed Kila felt the criticism that Wen was thinking but not saying. She should have suspected his purse was light based on where she'd found him. A wealthy man at Critt Sanglo's was only there to buy pleasures he dared not seek inside the city walls. That meant Keel had gone there with only the coin he was willing to spend—or have stolen.

"He also carried a sack," she said.

"Ah. Now I understand." He coughed again, but this time there was a laugh in it too. Laughing always made him cough. "Curiosity will kill you someday, sister."

It was true. No point in arguing. Any locked box or sealed bag was an irresistible lure to her. She couldn't help it. "There was something interesting in the sack."

"Do tell."

"An animal of some kind." She described it as best she remember. "It was dark on the roof."

A stirring of blankets came from across the little den. Light suddenly flared as Wen tore a flashtaper. Kila winced. The orange light underlit Wen's face, made hollows of his cheeks and eyes. He put it to the fishoil lantern. The weak light flickered and a coil of stinky black smoke lifted from the glass chimney. Kila opened their window, which was nothing more than a hand-sized hole covered with a board on a nail. She pivoted it up so that some of the smoke would lift out.

Wen blinked at her, face haggard with exhaustion. His eyes drifted to her wet clothes, now hanging from the low rafters to dry. She angled her face away to shadow the scrape on her cheek. "Do you know where the animal is now?" he asked.

"It ran off. Could be anywhere."

"Pity." He flopped back into his blankets. No bed, no mattress here. Just piles of rags and blankets. Some of it scavenged from Terriside rubbish heaps, some of it stolen from clotheslines. "What you described is a cat."

Now Kila sat up, holding her blanket to her throat. "What? Are you sure?"

"I saw one once. Came in on a ship from across the Ansin Ocean. From the Colony."

Kila gritted her teeth and bumped her forehead with her fist. Now her failure was complete. And now the Keel boy's purpose in Gristenside was clear. He wasn't going to Gristenside at all. He been headed to the Cathedral of Til to collect the bounty.

"Two gold skillets," she said. "I let two gold just walk away. It's no different than taking two skillets out of that sack and throwing them off the roof."

"You didn't know, sister. You've never seen a cat. Don't punish yourself for ignorance, learn from it."

That last bit was advice their father had repeated on many occasions. Kila had given him plenty of reasons to utter it. She knew Wen was trying to be his usual gentle self, but she only heard criticism.

She rolled away from his gaze, facing the rough plank wall of their little home. Their pathetic refuge. When Kila had moved them here after they'd been kicked out of their previous hovel for failure to pay rent. Wen had tried to cheer her up by saying it was cozy, like a little den. In truth, it was a six foot by six foot cell. Drafty, walls so thin she could hear the old man on the other side snoring. The floors had so many gaps that lantern light from the family below them leaked through in narrow beams. Their cooking smells also rose up to fill their space with burnt onion and fish.

It was the best Kila had been able to secure. Wen was too sick to steal. And what coin she did collect went mostly to his medicine and food. She'd started stealing food on occasion too, slipping through kitchen doors and lifting loaves and roast chickens. But going into a home or tavern kitchen was riskier than rolling a drunken mark. There were lots of knives in kitchens, and if someone happened to block her escape . . .

Wen's wheezes increased, but he didn't say anything further. He extinguished the fish oil lantern and the blessed darkness returned.

A cat. She'd had a cat in her grasp and she'd let it get away. Two skillets gone. That would have paid a ten-day's rent, two tens of Wen's medicine, and two meals a day to go with it.

Pitying yourself won't feed you, nor will hating yourself protect you, Father used to say. She grasped those words and tried to draw strength from them. Tomorrow she'd go looking for the cat, though somebody else would surely find it first. She had no idea if cats were sensible enough to hide or not.

"What else happened," Wen said.

"Huh?" How could he know that she was withholding something? But that was Wen. Sensitive to her moods and silences. It was as though he possessed some unthinking mercus sensitivity of his own, a kind that heard her deepest thoughts.

"Tell me."

"The Keel boy cried murder. He was right at the Harridan Gate. A Watch patrol must have heard. They came right away. They might have seen me." A safe lie. Her face was already known to the Watch.

"Ah," he said. And there was real disappointment in the sound. For she had failed at the one thing he'd asked of her.

No witnesses.

"Is that all?" he asked, already forgiving her.

"Yes. That's all."

There was only one person in the world Kila trusted. And as she strained to sleep in the heavy darknesss, she hated herself for lying to him.

6

LET HIM GO, SWEETIE

Dawn had banished the rain, leaving a clear blue sky and a breeze so fresh that the world felt washed clean. The failure of the previous night was fading like a bad dream. The only evidence of it was an abrasion on her cheek. Even small wounds could become corrupted if left unclean. She'd done her best to rinse it from the drinking water she and Wen collected in a pail, but she didn't trust it.

She'd tried to sneak out this morning, but there was no slipping out on Wen. He had probably known she was injured when she got home last night. He didn't press her for any explanation, but urged her to go see Finta. And so she would. Thing was, Finta charged for her services and Kila had no money. The old lady would probably help her in return for a promise, but Kila hated being in debt. She already owed five toll pails. Which was why she now stood on the Sorrows trying not to look like the pickpocket she was about to be.

In truth, picking pockets was not her strongest skill. Wen was the best she'd ever seen at lifting purses. He could steal your eyes and you'd think the sun had blinked out of existence before you suspected him. The trick for beginners was to do one's thieving amongst crowds. You needed the press of the throng as an excuse to brush into people. It was that contact that allowed your fingers to unbutton a pouch or dip into a loose pocket. In fact, you wanted the mark to feel the contact, because it allowed you to push their attention toward a distraction of your choosing. Namely, at a person you claimed had shoved you.

The morning crowds were on the Street of Sorrows in force. Youngsters off to market to fetch lists of necessities for their mothers, tradesmen going to and fro on their errands, merchants unloading wares from wagons, and all manner of scribes, bookkeepers, and law-speakers on their way to snug offices where they charged hard coin for their special knowledge. As far as Kila could tell, their primary skill was using up ink. She couldn't think of a worse way to live than spending a day bent over a ledger and marking in figures and ciphering up totals.

To pick a mark from this crowd required a discriminating eye. It required experience to know where a portly landlord stowed his coin. Such usually carried a bag of small coin, plugs to pay carpenters and trashhaulers or odd jobsmen. Always secured to a belt, with two buttons. Landlords were terrible marks.

Law-speakers kept gold in their pockets, ready to toss to barmen. Such were always conducting business in inn common rooms. Their purses were tight little pouches, often tucked at the small of their back and inside the high waistbands of their baggy trousers. That's why people said, "You'll get a coin from a law-speaker before you'll get a secret from me.".

Tradesmen carried less coin, but they also could spare less, so Kila and Wen didn't like robbing them. Donse Masters surely had larger purses, but they could also curse your bones with the mercus. Only a fool would try stealing from one of them.

Kila was looking for merchants and "income lords." The true lords of Starside—called Radiants— had shoestring relatives all across the tidy neighbor-hoods in Upper Terriside. Some were granted annual stipends, allowing them to live lazy and free. These were called income lords, but never to their faces.

Such folk wore looser tunics and trousers. Some even still wore hose, a style not popular for a hundred years or more. They carried "day purses," which they filled from fat coin boxes kept in their cellars. Or so Kila had been told once.

In any case, income lords were the marks she preferred. Trouble was, her concentration was failing her. It wasn't just the burning scrape on her cheek either. She kept discovering her head turned to look upslope. There was nothing there. Just the Street of Sorrows winding its way up the tiered city.

"Hey girl. Move along," barked a shopkeeper. He stood in his door behind her. Apron over his shabby vest and kneeloons.

"I'm on the street," she said, not bothering to look at him.

"You stink worse'n a swire hog in a flim gorn."

Any other day and she'd find a way to pay him back for that. She'd show him a flim gorn! But there was no time for petty vengeance. She moved up the street, and in doing so caught a whiff of her own smell. The man was right. She needed a wash. Her stink was going to make her task harder. People already looked at her askance. Her shirt of quilted rags and her cropped trousers were all the tells anyone here would need to know she was from Cheapgate. Add to that her filthy bare feet, and she might as well have been a scream-clown for the way folks recoiled when the saw her.

Throwing her hands up, she resigned herself to more debt. Abandoning the pickpocketing project, she ghosted into an alley and wended cross-slope toward the Divide.

The Divide was the one structure that dominated everything in the city. Even more than the Citadel, which was perched high up to the west. The morning sun glinted from the perfectly even top of the enormous wall. Made of seamless black stone, it was so tall that some parts of the city never escaped its shadow. It ran from the Citadel to the docks and then another five miles out to sea where it joined to the Sea Bastion.

As she made her way toward Ranci Park, she couldn't help but stare up at the impossibly tall barrier. On the other side lay Moonside. A few frigate birds were soaring over the wall now, not needing to flap their wings for the strength of the wind.

Well below the Divide and running parallel to it was the Starside Wall. It was fortified with hoardings and small towers where the Watch sometimes posted men with spyglasses. They would look down at the city to spy on people. Kila hated them on principle.

Father had said the Starside Wall had been built more recently than the Divide. A canal ran between the two walls. People said it was another measure to keep people from getting to Moonside. Kila wasn't so sure about that. In her fantasies, the walls were to keep something from getting out of Moonside. But whatever it was, it wasn't people. That whole side of the once unified city was sequestered, sealed off on all sides. Only Her Enlightened Majesty knew what lay within it, and maybe not even her.

Ranci Park was a sparsely treed green on a corner lot. Kila traipsed over the soggy autumn leaves. A quick hop over a wrought iron fence landed her in Finta's back garden. Kila was careful to tiptoe through the chard and squash vines. Finta stood at her back door, already smiling. "You're late."

To say that Finta Sahng's face was wrinkled was like saying the ocean was wet or that the Honor Mountains were tall. Finta's face was made of wrinkles. Yet there was fine beauty there. She had to be at least a hundred years old. Her prominent cheeks and firm jaw were strong from long years of smiling. And though she had never shed the black of mourning for the husband she'd lost fifty years prior, she had allowed her white hair to flow loose and free as a spring maid's. Kila pecked the woman's dry cheek and slipped into her fragrant little home shop.

"Late? I wasn't even planning to come here this morning."

"No? But surely Wen needs more of his tincture. It's on the table."

Finta's little kitchen was warm and well it by a broad south-facing window. Banked coals in the hearth warmed a kettle that already had a curl of steam rising. Dried herbs hung from the ceiling in tidy bunches. The air itself tasted like tea.

"Sorry I stink," Kila said, rubbing her elbows.

"Sit, child."

Kila sat, but she couldn't tolerate any misunderstanding with Finta. "Before you pour me tea, you need to know I'm already five plugs in debt to the roofway. I'm working on it, but I've had a run of bad luck."

Finta brought cups anyway and poured Kila a minty brimful. "Tell me about your brother."

"He'd not too good, no offense to your tincture. It does sooth his cough. But it makes him sleepy. He doesn't go out of the den often. Too much lying about can't be good for him."

Finta nodded sagely. "You understand that I cannot answer my own debts if you don't pay yours?"

"I do. I'm not here for Wen's medicine. Not yet. I'm here for my own face. It burns like Kil's fire."

Finta fetched a tiny wooden box from a cabinet. "This I can spare you now if you promise two plugs by Tilsday. Oxweed and tinbalm is plentiful for for the gathering if you know where to look." She tore a flash-taper and lit a candle. "You'd best let me look at."

The woman's gnarled fingers were strong and warm as they took hold of Kila's head and tilted her face to the light. Finta hummed thoughtfully as she applied her salve.

"Have you ever seen a cat?" Kila asked.

Finta's stopped mid swipe and peered into Kila's eyes. "Why do you ask?"

"I just thought you might have. Wen says he saw one once. Says they look sort of like a small hound, but more delicate."

"They look like hounds as much as cows look like horses," Finta said. There was a hard edge to her tone, but her fingers remained tender. "Cats were common enough before the Way of Til declared them a scourge. The true scourge is the increase in rats ever since the cats were taken. Now, you let that dry. Wash it with clean water—warm if you can come by it—and apply more salve at bedtime."

Kila thanked the old woman and accepted a tiny little wooden tube. The salve had cooled her cheek and relieved the prickly pain entirely. "You'll have your two plugs by Tilsday. But I'll try to be back sooner than that, with payment for Wen's tincture too."

She had gotten as far as Finta's door when the old woman said, "I had a cat. A neighbor stole him, gave him to the Donse Masters." There was no kindness in her voice now.

"Oh, I didn't know." Kila closed the door behind her and made her way back to the Sorrows. She knew her face didn't look any better, but at least the discomfort was gone. But now she felt discontented. She hadn't expected Finta to think kindly of cats. In truth, she'd hoped the old woman would give her an idea of where to look for the one she'd so stupidly let escape.

It was known that Finta had contrary ideas about a lot of things. It was why a healer of such skill was living in the poorest quarter of Terriside. As far as Kila knew, the woman was only a few coins from losing her little shop and being forced into a Cheapsgate shack herself.

By the time Kila had gotten back to the bustling junction of the Sorrows and Filiday Street, she'd put the question of Finta's cat behind her. The salve on her cheek seemed to have stoked the fires of her mind, for she felt a surge of energy in her limbs. Even her eyesight was sharper, almost like when the mercus vision was coming over her.

An hour had passed since she'd left for Finta's, now the sun angled into the Sorrows more directly, reducing the shadows. The chances of spotting a rich drunkard at this hour were low. It was even more imortant that she choose someone who was already distracted. She dismissed the lady ahead of her with her market basket hooked on an elbow. Her clothes were fine, but the basket was mounded with greens and potatoes. She had already spent her purse. Same problem with the man with the limp. She knew his boots alone cost three gold skillets, and his tunic was embroidered in a very new style. Thread of gold glistened on his collar. She and Wen had noted this detail was common in men who spent their coin to appear richer than than they were. Invariably their purses were flat.

She continued to scan and reject marks. They were either too fast or too thin or walked alone or were guarded by armed men or simply appeared too dangerous in their posture.

And then she spotted one of the young rogues she'd fought the night before. It was the ugly one with the lank pelt of black hair and the evil eyebrow. He was talking idly with a girl with a bundle of washing in her arms. She was trying to break off the conversation, but the fool either didn't notice or he didn't care. What was his name? Something like "fool" or "fellow."

Kila crossed the street and loitered just close enough to hear what he was saying.

". . . all that effort and do you know what she did?"

The girl shook her head and stepped back, making a half-turn to leave.

"She let it out and it ran away. Can you believe that? Two gold skillets and she let it go."

"That's strange," the girl said. "So you *don't* have it."

"Not yet. My partner knows where it's holed up. Where do you live? I'll stop by once we have it bagged up. I'll let you see it before we go collect our coin."

The girl looked past him and locked eyes with Kila. Seeing Kila's fury, she squawked and dashed away, losing a sock from her bundle. Fallo took a few steps after her, but thought better of it. He turned and saw Kila looking at him. He didn't recognize her. "Ah, and I though it was *my* face that scared her off. You ought to have someone look at that scrape." He squinted, which bunched his single caterpillar of an eyebrow over his nose. A smile of crowded teeth showed genuine good humor as he came toward her. "Say, you're pretty under all that Cheapsgate grease, aren't you? Peculiar looking, but pretty in your own way. I'd say if you healed that cheek and washed your hair and changed your clothes and gained a couple stone of flesh, you'd be the prize dance at any ball in Upper Terrisde. What's your name?"

"Kila," she said, closing the gap. He misinterpreted her approach for actual interest in him, and his strange smile grew bigger. It didn't widen, as would be usual for most people. Rather it stretched vertically, showing his gums. His dark eyes squinted and a splotchy blush crept up his throat.

Abruptly he went pale and his mouth constricted into a tight circle. "Kila? Uh oh!" He turned and ran. Kila went after him. Passersby called for civility, a few simply watched. One even hollered encouragement to Kila, assuming Fallo was a thief. But a laughing fat man with one arm called, "Let him go, sweetie. You can do better!"

These words burned her ears and she was tempted to turn around and relieve him of his remaining arm. But she'd left the rusty dagger she'd taken from the boys in the den.

Anger propelled her now. That villain had been spying on her! He'd watched her open the sack, and had seen the cat slip away. All that after she had warned him away from her territory.

And she hadn't noticed.

That more than anything else singed her backside. How many times had Father—and Wen—reminded her that she was not the only thief in Starside? And on any given night there were sure to be a few more skulking about.

The ugly boy had longer legs and more power in them. It appeared he knew the allies and sidestreets as well as she did. He bounded over a high garden fence and by the time Kila got over it, he was gone. She stood there, panting, looking all around for where he might have gone. There was no way he had crossed the entire garden and gotten over the opposite fence.

A shriek erupted in the house, followed by the baying of at least a half dozen small dogs. A door slammed. A woman cried out.

He'd cut through the house! Kila dashed down the little sideyard, squeezed through a hedge, and came out into a little gated front yard filled with fuzzy dogs. They yelped and clawed at a wrought iron gate. Fallo clung to the top of it, pants caught on a spear-shaped finial. He spotted Kila, smirked and flung himself over the top. His trousers ripped from seat to the ankle. He ran off, whooping with glee, tatters of one trouser leg flapping.

Something heavy clanged into the fence next to

Kila's head. A cast iron skillet. "Get away! Thief! Murderer! Murderer! Help me! HELP ME! MURDER!"

The housemother continued to scream from inside her house. A rattle of pots and pans gave Kila all the warning she needed that the woman would soon reappear armed with more iron. The little dogs caught wind of her and gave pursuit. She was forced back through the hedge and over the garden wall to escape their nasty little rat-killing fangs. The housemother continued to roust the entire neighborhood. Kila ghosted away, furious at Fallo's escape. Furious that he knew where the cat was and was on the verge of capturing it.

Even worse, she was furious that she'd allowed herself to be distracted by him this morning when her job was to lift a purse on the Sorrows. What matter was a two-skillet cat anyway? If she was patient and applied her skills carefully, she might lift twice that this very afternoon.

And so she returned to the Sorrows for the third time, committed to stealing well and to forgetting all about Fallo and the ridiculous cat. He could have it, assuming he truly knew where it was. The way he tried to charm her and other girl, she figured he was all boast and no toast.

She unclenched her jaw and rocked her head side to side to loosen her neck. She talked to herself a bit, and reminded herself that she knew what she was doing. It was simple pride that had allowed her to be distracted. No more.

As if Pol herself were listening to Kila's thoughts,

her luck changed. A short, stout man barged out of a law-speaker's office, waving a crumple of papers and shouting about taking something up with Radiant Gilok. His coat was of thick, fine wool. But not the black that wealthy merchants perferred. This was a deep blue, with buttons so shiny they short flares into Kila's eyes. Beneath were ballooning pants tucked into small ankle boots. They were the sort of shoes men wore when they planned to be indoors from morning until bedtime. His bald pate shone in the sun, but it was red with fury.

A trim young man came out after him, imploring His Excellency to stay and talk things over. But the stout man was having none of it. He stormed off, ripping the papers to little bits and tossing them over his shoulder in a flurry of scraps. His coat was was unfastened and it blew back a bit with all his arm flailing. Kila beheld a fat pouch dangling rather obscenely beneath his protruding belly.

Her mouth went a bit dry at the prospect of the take. Her heart galloped. But her eyesight sharpened even more. After a few moments, there was nothing in the world but the man's stout body and his shining bald head. Kila followed him as he stormed upslope along the Sorrows. He continued to shout occasionally. People of all trades and classes gave him a wide berth. Even better, his tantrum drew their attention away from Kila, so she was able to get much closer to him than she would usually dare.

Already her mind was ahead of the man, thinking through the switchbacks of the Sorrows and where the crowds were the densest. She still wanted to do a bump and grab rather than a shadow and roll. Daytime muggings were bad thiefcraft. His clothes suggested wealth, but she could not understand why he was walking. A man like this should have an atlen-drawn carriage standing by at all times. Odd. He must have come downslope in a hired hack.

Yes. And that's why he was raising his hand right now and shouting at a passing driver. He was trying to get a hack to take him home. That would never do. Kila was fast, but nobody could keep up with an atlen team. Pol favored Kila again, for the driver passed by without slowing. The stout lord stomped and swore, then continued uphill.

The Sorrows climbed to Chance's Corner ahead, a widening in the street that leveled into an oblong plaza. Cart vendors were already shouting their offer-ings, of soups or steamed clams. A line of empty hire carriages was usually arranged on the far side of the Corner. This was it. This was where she had to make the take.

Kila ran ahead of her mark, taking a wide circle around the crowd. One thing she knew about rich, stout men, they did not walk farther than they had to. He would bull through the throngs and expect everyone to make way. He would not find his fellow citizens cooperative here.

Kila trotted along, trying to look like a girl sent on an errand. Whether folk believed her act or not was impossible to say. Most ignored her entirely. There was too much else to look at, too many people to talk too,

too much food to eat. The smell of it tied Kila's stomach in a disgruntled knot. She hadn't had a meal since this time yesterday. Even more reason to pluck that purse and be gone.

Judging that she was far enough ahead of him, she took a hard angle toward the line of carriages. The hack captain gave her a leery looking over before turning his attention back to the crowd. His job was to guide folk to a conveyance, not to police vagrants. Kila spotted the bench she remembered. It was occupied. No matter, she went to a little table that one of the bordering eateries had put out for fine weather dining. One hop and she was straddling two women's tea and cakes and peering over the sea of faces. Her mark was a barge among rowboats. He shoved folk aside as he stormed ahead. People cursed him. But when they turned to confront him for his rudeness, they snapped their teeth together and said nothing. They recognized him.

One of the women seated at Kila's table swatted her leg. "Get down from there! What have we come to in this city?" She twisted in her chair. "Freddi! Freddi! Get this filthy thing off our biscuit medley!"

But Kila was done with the table. She jumped down and wove into the crowd. It was easy to arrow straight for her mark by following the yelps and curses. There he was, right in front of her. His brows made a vee over the bridge of his nose. His lips were bunched up in a sneer. His face and head were flushed and shining with sweat.

The mercus vision swept over her so suddenly, she

stumbled. A man accidentally elbowed her in the gut. She bent double. Her ears filled with conversation, with rustling clothes, with the jingle of coins in a fat purse. Her nose was stuffed with the smells of steaming clams, onion, and baking bread. The noisome odor of a far off rubbish heap blended in, replacing her appetite with nausea. The stones of the street revealed their grit under her feet.

She straightened by will alone, pulling in a breath. Metal glowed everywhere. Buttons, daggers, fences, sewer grates, downspouts, and coins. There were coins all around her. But the greatest concentration of them was passing her by. She lunged, shouldering into the man's padded body. Her hand found the purse, climbed up the leather tie to the ivory button that held it fast. A twist and flip with her thumb and—

It didn't come loose.

"Get off me, nasty slattern!" he said, shoving her hard. Her grip on his purse pulled his hips around. His face crumpled into black fury. "Thief! I'll have your hands. I'll have them on a plate!" He slapped her face, setting flame to her injured cheek.

Still she did not let go. Her fingers searched for the button as she fended off another slap. She went to her knees.

"Let go!" he cried, kicking out and slapping with both hands. He was a frenzy of open-handed attacks.

Her own anger rose, along with no small amount of panic. Her grip on the purse was that of a girl clinging to a ledge above a great fall. Her fingers burned. Suddenly the leather cord parted and purse was hers.

"Murder!" the man cried. His meaty palm smashed the back of her head, driving her head-first into a lady's backside.

"Horrid tramp!" the man cried. Something struck her ribs.

It was the man's foot. His tiny foot in its ridiculous indoor shoe. She scurried away on hands and knees, gulping for air. She squeezed through legs, shouldered into another lady's belly, then bounded to her feet. The overwhelming assault of the mercus vision and the accompanying heightening of all her other senses made the Street of Sorrows lurch and tilt.

She broke free of the crowd. A chorus of insults followed her, for in her flight she had knocked over several bystanders and had startled twice as many nearly out of their shirts. But chaos worked to her advantage. So many were so angry that none cared to listen to the stout man crying "murder" about his lost purse. In fact, he couldn't even bully his way back out of their ranks, for they were too busy raising fists and calling shame on Kila and her ancestors. Such insults were nothing compared to the average friendly conversation in Cheaspgate.

Grinning, she turned to sprint away.

A hand grabbed the collar of her shirt, a rip tore through the air. She landed on her backside, hard. The purse twisted from her grip. "Thankee, luv." A stocky man with filthy unshaven cheeks smiled at her. She reached to snatch the purse back.

"Ah ah ah! This isn't yer prop'rty." He turned away and called for the stout man Kila had just robbed. No doubt he was counting on a nice reward for his good deed.

"Best be runnin, lass," he called back to her.

She scrambled to her feet, growling. But like any threatened animal, instinct pressed her to flee rather than fight. Empty-handed, and aching, she fled Chance's Corner. She ran until she could no longer hear the shouts of anger behind her. Constantly weaving downslope, she had to hold the collar of her shirt together to keep it from falling off her shoulder. When she was certain there was no pursuit, she pulled up in a grassy park and spilled herself onto her back. The mercus vision remained, taunting her with the glow of metal all around. But all she could see was the gold-filled purse so cruelly stolen from her.

7

ON THE BRIM

"Yes, Seer Hargothe," Dunne Skyll said. He drew the curtain of the sedan chair shut, taking care to overlap the folds to keep daylight out. Even with no eyes, the Hargothe was painfully sensitive to light on his skin. It didn't make sense. But it didn't have to.

They had come to Chance's Corner, a popular plaza at a bend in the Street of Sorrows. The smell of cart vendor stews and sweetbakes filled the air. The odors annoyed the Hargothe. Gauging the wind, Skyll decided the old man would be spared most of the smells if he were positioned below the plaza.

The men bearing the chair were armsmen from Radiant Sinnon's barracks, but they were assigned indefinitely to serve the Way of Til in return for secret favors known only to Highest Chilow. These men were not accustomed to being made beasts of burden, and it had taken repeated instruction to keep them walking in step. The Hargothe blamed Skyll for every tilt and jolt of the sedan chair.

The chair itself was a plush lounge. The seer lay supine upon it, shoulders and head raised on pillows. The curtains were black velvet lined with several layers of silks to blot out all light. The chair rode upon two long, gilded poles that rested upon the armsmen's shoulders. Such conveyances were popular in some southern cities, but they were a novelty in Starside. The wealthy here perferred atlen-drawn carriages. Starside was a vast city and travel distances were too great to be covered on foot.

The Hargothe couldn't abide the rattle of a carriage, so he had to be carried. He had directed them to come here. He said Sigh had recently been aglow upon the mercusine in this very spot. Dunne Skyll scanned the crowd. It was all merchants, scribes, and ledgermen. Ink on fingers and pale complexions abounded. Idle women were out in little gaggles, enjoying the fine sunlight with an open air repast.

He spotted a squad of the city Watch. Wrinkling his nose, he approached them. Their captain noticed him and broke from his conversation with a plump-bottomed woman in a torn skirt. "Donse Master," the man said. He had the usual swollen neck and nose of a Watch leader, used to too little walking and too much drinking.

"There was a girl here," Dunne Skyll said. "Filthy, skinny. A thief of some ability."

"Yes, yes. Kila Sigh is well known to us. She just

robbed Radiant Portino. We know she lives in Cheaps-gate. We'll have her in the Westbunk by day's end."

"You will do no such thing."

"But Radiant Portino wants her—"

"I will have Highest Chilow speak with Portino. You will withdraw your men from the search. This is a matter for the Way of Til."

The Watch supposedly answered to the crown, and not to the Way of Til. But of all the institutions of government in the city, the Watch was the least compe-tent and most corrupt. In truth, the Watch avoided confrontations if at all possible. Skyll's coin crossed the captain's palm and vanished into a pocket.

But the Watch also had to maintain the appearance of doing their job. A broad daylight purse grab could not go unanswered, especially with so many witness, and even more so with a Radiant as victim. And so Dunne Skyll was forced to perform for the crowd. "You have done well here today. I'm impressed that you already know where the thief is hiding. Til favors those who protect the innocent and persecute the guilty." He made a big show offering the blessing of Til's hand and then jerked his head. The man under-stood and summoned his men. They tromped off downslope, as if going to fetch Sigh. They would likely stop at the next tavern and call the day's work done.

Dunne Skyll went to report to the Hargothe. The man shushed him. "She's moving. I must listen."

And so the armsmen stood under the weight of his sedan chair and Dunne Skyll sweated in the sun, head wound prickling. Abruptly his mind filled with a hissed voice. *She's downslope.*

The Hargothe rarely spoke to him directly in this way. Skyll had been too hot moments before, but now his skin thrilled with cold horror. He didn't know if he should try to think back an answer or not. He didn't really know how to do it. So he motioned for the armsmen to move and led them downslope, hoping against hope that the Hargothe never did that trick again.

But he did.

She's in Lower Terrisde, the Hargothe sent. *She's not fully awake to her power, but close. Very close. Yessss. She balances on the brim.*

8

THE GRUNTING PIG

Lying on her back in the grass, Kila imagined unfastening the leather cord and pulling the mouth of the purse open. It was supremely fine with a soft velvet lining. She imagined dumping the contents onto the grass and delighting in the musical tinkling of coin striking coin. The mercus glow would overlay each gold skillet, silver, and copper plug. It was dazzling. She counted as she put each one back in the purse.

Fifteen gold skillets, eight silver skillets, four silver plugs, and twelve copper plugs. She hefted the make-believe purse in her hands, squeezed it, sniffed it. Then she dumped it all back out and counted it again, this time feeling each coin, savoring the unimaginable wealth that was now hers. This would get them through Winternight, and maybe beyond.

"Kil's eyes in a bucket!" she said, opening her eyes and watching a lone cloud drift against the blue. So close.

Her belly gave a little twist, reminding her that she had neglected her own needs far too long. Remembering the cart vendors in Chance's Corner, she decided she'd have to risk a quick run-and-grab to get her lunch. Too many people had watched her run off from Chance's to try it there. A fine clear day like today, the cart vendors would be out all over the Sorrows. Father had always said daytime snatches were a bad practice. Today's failure surely had proved him right.

But if she waited until dark, she would be weaker and Finta would go to bed. She meant to have Wen's medicine tonight. He had not looked well when she'd left.

Her hunger got her thinking about crusty bread and thick creamy soup. Hoisting herself to her feet, she knotted the rip in her collar to secure her shirt a bit tighter. The safest place for a run and grab was at the bottom of the Sorrows. So she made her way deeper into Lower Terriside and slipped into the shadows at the edge of Cheaps Market, a gritty plaza right where the Cheaps let into the city. The Grunting Pig occupied one corner. A massive stone tavern with three huge doors. The one-eyed tough who watched the front entry gave her a skeptical looking over. She ducked deeper into the alley. The Pig would let in anybody who could pay as long as you didn't bother the other patrons. But Kila didn't have a coin to flash, so the tough wouldn't let her in.

As expected a bunch of mismatched tables had been brought out for folk to enjoy the day. There were a few seamen, easily identified by the tails they made of their long hair. Metal jewelery sparkled in her mercus vision, dangling from ear and nose, encircling fat, calloused fingers. Stealing from a sailor was asking for a drubbing. They strong, agile, and quick to anger when their shoretime was disrupted.

A shabby man in coat and collar was hunched over a platter in the center of the gathering of tables. He had the look of fallen wealth. Merchants sometimes drew Pol's ire. Nobody liked them, not even the gods. His pewter mug still foamed at the top. He was picking at his meal with pinched fingers.

Kila walked toward him, keeping her eyes up the street. Just walking easily. Enjoying the day. Yes. She was just looking for a friend. They planned to meet here before walking up the Sorrows together. Nothing to be suspicious of. A Cheapsgate girl, no doubt about that. Why did they let her through the gate? Ah, but what can be done? The Watch guards are all corrupt. Everybody knows that.

A faded banner hung from the gables of tavern, of a smiling pig in a helmet, holding aloft a foaming mug in one hoof.

Kila wove through the mostly-vacant benches. The patrons didn't look up. They were too deep in their own feeding to worry about a filthy street urchin. She knew the proprietor by reputation, a curt man called Rammelstone. He kept a clean establishment, but whispers told of grimy happenings in his cellars. This close to Cheapsgate, an odd mix of folk came through. Especially sailors and travellers. If you wanted to get large quantities of goods or people in or out of the city without notice or taxes, you might find Rammelstone's services of use.

The clerk was reading a book. It was flopped open on the table next to him. He was so engrossed in it, he wasn't even eating. Kila surveyed her escape route. She'd have to run straight ahead. The Cherry Bottom Inn was down there. She knew those alleys well because the sewer grate to Cheapsgate was tucked next to the Inn.

She rounded his table, paused and jerked back to look at the Cheaps. "Kil be a merry maiden! She's naked!"

The reading man looked up at her, saw her staring wide-eyed at the gate. He twisted in his chair. "Where? Where is she?"

Kila's feet beat stone as she fled, carrying the entire platter in her hands. Beer! She'd stolen beer. And stew. And bread. And butter! She couldn't believe her luck. Butter!

The alley shadows engulfed her as the man's cries rose weakly behind. She didn't look back. When fleeing a grab, you never look back. If you do, you'll twist up your feet and go face first into the ground.

Her mercus vision was alight. Wrought iron gates and fences blurred past her as she ran. She twisted down back lanes and took public stairwells upslope, breath heaving. Her keen ears caught no sounds of pursuit. Only a third of the beer had spilled, and even that was puddled on the platter. Kila was not above slurping up a bit of it. No she was not!

With new strength in her limbs, she slipped a bit north to an elnisian cemetery. It was overgrown with weeds and gnarled crabapple trees. There was a sunny patch on top of a carved stone tomb where she and Wen sometimes lazed on fine afternoons like this.

She sat down before her platter and inspected her meal. That fool clerk hadn't touched but a corner of the bread. The beer was still cold. She put her nose to the foam and sniffed. Wen didn't like her drinking beer, said it was a bad habit for thieves, who needed to keep their senses sharp at all times. But two beers a year could hardly be said to be a habit. Besides, he didn't need to know about it.

Kila tucked into her meal. Her first swallow of stew forced moan of pleasure from her. Flushing, she ducked her head and continued stuffing her face. The stew, the bread, the butter. It went down in bolts of ecstasy. She saved her beer for the end, forcing herself to take small swallows and enjoy it. She licked her finger and dabbed up the last crumbs of bread. Her belly hadn't been this full in a fortnight. The meal was almost enough to make up for the disaster in Chance's Corner. And there was this pewter mug. A smith could melt it down and rework it easily. She might get a copper or two for it.

As she slurped the last drop of beer from the platter, a tickle scurried up the back of her neck like a dozen harry little fingers.

Someone was watching her.

Taking the mug with her, she slipped down from the tomb and scanned the lane. Nothing. Most windows were curtained. All were dark. Nobody there. She didn't like this feeling. There was someone out there. Watching her.

Her eyes kept roving west, back upslope. Somebody was up there, looking at her. But that was impossible. Giving herself a shake she pushed the feeling away. She'd been in one spot too long, was all. She didn't dare go to the Cheaps Market any time soon, so she wended through alleys to the next leg of the Sorrows.

Pausing again in the shadows, she scanned faces, searching the little concealed areas she had used in the past to look for marks. Nothing there. She felt drawn to wander a bit down the street and see if she could spot whoever it was who was spying on her. The sensation was so heavy that she just knew someone was stalking her. Maybe that man who had taken her purse away. Lord Stouty Indoor Shoes might have hired him to get her.

Catching herself in the thought, she snorted. Instincts were one thing, but mysteriously *knowing* that someone was watching you stretched all reason. It had to be her imagination. After all, she'd robbed that man among a crowd and had been seen fleeing downslope. It only made sense that the Watch was searching for her. That had to be it. She was just jumpy.

What she had to do now was rack this pewter mug off for coin. She knew a smith who would take it off her hands and ask no questions. She'd hole up until dark. Then it was back to the roofway to stalk drunk marks with fat purses. She resolved that this time she wouldn't get hooked by curiosity over any sacks on shoulders. It was purses only and then ghost away into the night. Wen would just have to make it till morning.

She rubbed her belly and burped. The meal wasn't sitting well inside her. What was that line from the Holy Theb? "Ill gotten bread makes ill feeding." Ridiculous. Bread was bread as gold was gold. If you didn't have it, you had to get it. Simple as that.

Rather than go back to Cheapsgate, she decided to bend her course north and climb one of the dilapidated buildings in the Blasted Quarter. Nobody would look for her there because few were stupid enough to go into any of the ruins. But there were a couple of sturdy ones remaining, and Kila knew a perfect spot to take a day-long nap.

As she climbed an echoey stairwell in a building missing one entire wall, the mercus vision slipped away. By the time she got to the sun-drenched roof, she was yawning.

9

TWISTING AND GRABBING

anci Park had declined remarkably since Dunne Skyll had last been there. It must have been sixty years ago, back when Lower Terriside was a respectable quarter. The city's park groomers had given it up as a lost cause apparently. The grass was unkempt and brown. The cherry trees that had onced bloomed so gloriously here had gone feral, their limbs twisting and grabbing each other. The year's fruits were all gone, stolen by Terrisiders who had no sense of public pride at all.

The armsmen stood as still as they could, faces stony beneath their burden. In truth the Hargothe himself added no appreciable weight. But the chair and poles were heavy, especially after the long walk downslope. A dozen acolytes had been waiting in this park when Skyll and the Hargothe had arrived. They bore buckets of steaming water, towels, fresh robes, and a heavy ceramic pot of soup. They motioned the armsmen to set down the chair. "Gently now!" they mouthed. One went inside while the others passed in the buckets and robes and towels and soup.

That they knew to be here at all meant the Hargothe had used his vile mind-speaking trick on one of them. They attended him with utter devotion. When the lead man came out of the curtained chair, he wore a worried expression. He conferred with the others and shook his head. They collected their empty bucket and wet towel and half-empty soup jug and trudged away, giving Dunne Skyll parting glowers. As a Donse Master, he warranted more respect than he was paid. They should have sought his permission before leaving. They hadn't.

He let them go. He had greater worries at the moment.

She has gone north, the Hargothe sent. *Take me to the Blasted Quarter.*

And that was all the instruction Dunne Skyll would receive. He bade the men pick up their burden. He hoped capturing Sigh was worth this effort. After his first encounter he was starting to think it best to kill her. The Hargothe was powerful enough as it was, and Skyll did not care to imagine what he'd become if he had Sigh on a tether.

10

THIS SCRAWNY THING

When Kila emerged from her nap, the sun was still too high to begin her stalk along the Sorrows. So she lazed in its warmth, dangling her legs over the drop. From this high vantage, she could see the whole city, sloping steeply down from the Citadel on her right to Cheapsgate on her left. The Ansin Ocean was a gray, infinite sheet beyond the docks.

Straight ahead lay Terriside, tiled rooves, climbing tier by tier, growing richer with each step toward Gristenside. She could make out Chance's Corner from here. Beyond it the city rambled until stopping dead, just short of the Starside Wall. The enormous Divide towered a third again as tall. Black, seamless, and without variation along its length. The sun was bending toward the peaks of the Honor Mountains just behind the highest spires of the Citadel. People said Her Enlightened Majesty, Ell LiMinluit, kept an office at the top of one of those towers. Rather stupid, in Kila's judgement. How many stairs would she have to climb just to get up there? A thousand? Completely impractical.

The breeze tickled her collarbone and she remembered the tear in her shirt. She shucked it off and inspected the damage. Not too bad. The rags she'd made it from were tough strips of sail cloth, tarpaulin, and wagon cover. The stitching had torn, was all. She could mend it easily with needle and netline later. She managed to knot it more securely and slipped it back over her scrawny frame. Already her meal was gone, absorbed into the endless pit of her hunger.

She would steal a purse tonight, maybe two. In fact, she decided she would rob until she had no less than the two skillets she'd lost when that stupid cat got away from her. And if she ended up with three or four skillets, maybe she'd buy a new shirt for herself. And a proper belt so she could carry that rusty dagger she'd taken off the boys last night.

But it rankled having to pay for clothes. It was why she had made her own shirt. If you stole clothes off of drying lines, people might recognize them. The rag-and-bone man wouldn't give a Cheapsgater a chipped plug for stolen clothes. But that wasn't the true reason she didn't steal clothes. She didn't like the idea of wearing other people's things. Things that had been up against their skin. Wen thought it a silly aversion, but she didn't care what he thought. It was her skin.

Rested and fed as she was, she began to get antsy.

She didn't like waiting around when there was work to be done. Father always said that the life of a lazy thief was short and humiliating. Success in any endeavor took work.

Descending from the ruined building warmed her sore muscles. After tonight she'd give herself a day or two of rest. All this running about and getting knocked down was starting to tell. Later she would rub some of Finta's salve on her muscles and see if that helped.

She jerked to a stop just outside the entryway. There were men out on the street, just where there shouldn't be any. Armsmen in helms, with swords on their hips. A Donse Master stood with them. His gray hair ruffled in the wind. A white beard. It was him! They were looking all about, searching.

She ghosted back into shadows.

The men kept looking around at the buildings, arguing with the Donse Master in raspy whispers. Their stiff necks told of suppressed impatience, or nervousness. They looked like men fed up with mistreatment. Good. *"Sow discord and your enemies will reap vengeance upon themselves."* Perhaps the Theb wasn't all nonsense.

She waited until they were all facing away before darting from her spot to put another ruined building between her and them. She wasn't too worried about the armsmen. They weren't carrying flickbows. As long as that Donse Master didn't see her, she was safe.

The Blasted Quarter was silent save for the occasional pebble falling away from a wall. The streets were cluttered with such debris. Nobody knew what had happened here save that it had happened during elnisian times. There was scant evidence of recent traffic, though Kila knew a few folk sheltered in the ruins despite the dangers. Some were just too proud to live in Cheapsgate. So they came here. And died.

She hustled along, casting the occasional backward look. Nobody came after her. Soon she was out of the quarter and into Smith's Row where forge fires dusted every surface with heavy soot. Her stop at Scivn Natch's shop lasted the time it took for her to wave the pewter mug with one hand and cup her other. He plopped two copper in her palm. She shook the coins and kept her hand open. He added a nicked plug and waved her off. She frowned and tossed him the mug.

Being rid of the mug made her feel lighter. It wasn't wise to carry stolen loot about. But racking that thing off boosted her spirits. Now that she'd had some time to think about it, she saw that her failure at Chance's Corner had been bad luck. Pol sometimes frowned, and nobody knew why. But Kila had done well for herself with the mug and the food. Father would have approved, except that she'd done it in daylight.

She watched her feet as she walked away from Smith's Row, lost once again counting the imaginary coins from the purse that had gotten way. It might have held even more than fifteen gold. The thought made her suck air through her teeth and bump her forehead with the heels of her hands.

Fifteen gold! She could have set aside a few toward her and Wen's dream of going into legitimate business. They both held to their Father's dream of setting up as licensed recovery agents. People would pay them to take back possessions that other people had stolen. But such licenses were expensive, and they couldn't apply for one until they had a shop. Recovery agents had to have some sort of business that masked their true operation. Everybody knew that.

Kila had no idea what that business might be, but whatever it was, it would require coin to stock the shelves. It was ridiculous that so many obstacles were thrown up to keep them from using their skills to help people. Not that Kila minded stealing. She and Wen never stole from anyone in Cheapsgate. They'd never steal from a soul who lived in Lower Terriside. What would be the point? Taking five copper plugs from a black-dressed old widow would do them little good, and it would mean the death of the old lady. People would find out if you did that sort of thing. Reputation was everything in Cheapsgate. The only sort who would rob a granny were the villains who worked for Dox Viller. Kila did not consider herself a villain.

Something was odd about this neighborhood.

She stopped and looked at the houses around her. This wasn't Lower Terriside. At some point in her amble she had turned her steps in the exact opposite direction she had intended to go. She was back in Upper Terriside, well west of Chance's Corner. She hadn't even noticed she was going upslope. She glanced at the sun. It was behind the mountains now, though the sky was still very light.

She twisted her head about to get her bearings. This wasn't an area she came to often. The being-watch feeling was gone, but something else pulled her attention now. Like an itch in her brain, unscratchable and irritating.

A sense of done-it-before came over her as she went down a quiet back lane. Walls to right and left guarded large gardens in back of stately homes. These were wealthy folk. Merchants and law-speakers and paper-shufflers who served in the Citadel.

Something was ahead. Something she needed to see. Her course bent south and she was again upon the Sorrows. And very near to where she'd been the previous night. Just over there was the mouth of the Harridan Gate.

She spotted him leaning against a wall beneath an overhang in front of an inn. The eyebrow, the flop of black hair. It was that rogue Fallo again. He had on different pants now, though they were much too big for his thin frame.

He was looking down the street, posture relaxed, but his eyes were alive and active. He was keeping watch. Kila backed into an alley, finding the deepest shadow from which to spy.

A lookout. No doubt about it. But for his position to be useful, his partner had to be close, within shouting distance. Kila decided to bide her time and watch.

The pull on her attention lifted her head and her

eyes to the rooftop above Fallo. Not much to see. Just a ledge concealing a flat roof beyond.

Fallo was doing his best not to look evil, and failing. "What an ugly face," Kila marveled.

A head popped into view above the ledge then disappeared. Somebody was up there. It had to be Fallo's partner. Kila glanced left and right, checking her guess. There was no doubt in her mind. That roof was where she'd let the cat out of the sack.

Would it have stayed so close after it ran off? If so, Fallo's partner was up there trying to capture it. Kila faded deeper into the alley and chose a route onto the roofway that would keep her hidden from the street. Thieves rarely used the roofway during the day unless they needed to travel fast. But there were paths one could take that kept mostly out of view. It took her a quarter of an hour to loop around to get behind Fallo and his friend. She finally got into position on the peaked roof of a the brewers' guild hall. From here she could survey the rooftop where the cat had gotten loose. And there was the ginger-haired boy. He was sitting with his back against a chimney. Ten paces in front of him was a dish. He had an empty sack over his knees.

The pull Kila had felt earlier was almost impossible to resist now. Her impulse was to go down and send the boy on his way. She stopped herself, instincts alive. She had been drawn here, as if by . . . not the mercus. But something outside of herself.

With that thought, the mercus vision struck again. This time she didn't waver as much. It helped that she wasn't in the middle of a purse lift amongst a huge crowd. Iron nailheads popped into view in the shake shingles beneath her. Scuppers and downspouts revealed themselves, even when blocked from view by brick and timber. The boy was not carrying a weapon, but he did appear to have a few coppers in a pocket.

Her vision went black. She put her hands down to keep herself from falling. The blindness flickered with bright flashes and blurs, like a nightscape lit up by lightning.

The darkness vanished and the world came back to her, bright and clear. But she was seeing from the wrong place—as if she were crouched across from the boy. The dish lay between them. It had meat in it. She could smell it. He was staring at her, hands slowly moving to open the sack.

But she wasn't across from the boy. Her feet and hands sensed the distinct roughness of the wood shingles of the guild hall roof. And even with her heightened senses, there was no way she should be able to smell what was in that dish from this distance.

The muscles along her flanks rippled, her legs tensed. The dish drew closer, as if she were crawling toward it. The boy stiffened, hands lifting the sack, fingers pulling the mouth of it wide apart. He stared right into her eyes.

Her vision snapped back to where it belonged. She wavered on the rooftop, her belly going all watery with nausea. The boy had not spotted her, all his attention focused on his quarry. The cat stalked toward the dish, dragging its belly, ears forward.

Beneath the fading daylight the cat's form wasn't so strange as it had been last night. Gone was the phantom silkyness of its vague shape. Now it simply looked like an animal. An elegant animal, but no odder than a peculiar breed of dog. It moved with supreme softness, inching toward the dish while keeping a keen eye out for any movement from the boy. Kila realized the pair had been at this game for a long while. And she would've bet a silver plug that the cat had gotten away with several morsels of meat already.

It was no different this time. The cat lunged, snatched, and dashed. The boy had barely gotten to his feet by the time the cat was bounding away with its prize. He didn't look particularly surprised by this. He went to the dish, prodded it with his toe.

Kila skidded down the guild hall roof and leapt the gap, landing softly on the boy's roof. He saw her coming but didn't move to run away. The way down was behind her. He lifted his chin, which was scraped as raw as her cheek. This was the boy who had attacked her last night. He was a bit bigger than her, but not by much. Red hair curled from under a knit cap. His skin was sunburned and covered with freckles.

Unlike his friend, he didn't offer any charming words or smiles. He simply dropped his head and seemed to resign himself to a confrontation. "I don't have any coin for you to steal," he said. His voice was firm, with the snappy enunciation of the well educated. Probably a runaway from some merchant house. Might even be the son of a minor tradesman. They all put their boys under tutors in hopes of making them bookkeepers, or to prepare them for a life in the Way of Til.

"You have at least three copper plugs," she said.

His faint brows lifted, but he made no motion to turn out his pockets. She didn't want his coins anyway. "Give me the sack. Go down and tell Fallo the cat is mine."

"You want it now? I watched you let it go."

"From where?"

"From the roof you just came off of. We watched you rob Raginalt Keel. We wanted to know what was in the sack. Fallo and I had a wager going."

"Who won?"

"Neither of us. Who would have thought it was a cat?"

"What makes you think it's a cat?"

"It looks like one."

This conversation was going nowhere. "What's your name?"

"Henley. And you're Kila Sigh."

"Well Hen, I warned you last night to stay out of my territory." She didn't have the dagger with her, so aggressive confidence would have to suffice.

"Don't call me Hen. And you can't claim all of Starside as your territory." He crossed his arms. "It's not reasonable."

Fallo's voice came from behind her. "Hey, you found me." He circled wide around her to join his friend. "Pol frowns with one side of her mouth and smiles with the other. Don't you think she'd clean up nicely, Hen?"

"Don't call me Hen. I don't see how Pol is smiling. The cat got the last of our giblets. I told you we should have set a box trap."

"You don't have to worry about that now," Kila said, motioning that the way was clear for them both to depart. "The cat is mine."

Fallo snorted. "The cat belongs to the cat. You'll never catch it. Come on, Hen. No reason to get more bruises over this. The bounty is too little to bother with anyway. Say, I'm hungry. I guess it's atlen eggs for us again."

The two left, strutting rather stupidly considering they were retreating from a lone girl smaller than either of them. This made Kila rather pleased with herself. She took Henley's spot at the chimney. She reckoned that she had plenty of time to wait for the cat before full night cleared the street for some stealing. And if she caught the cat, she'd have her self-imposed gold quota all bundled up in one go.

"You need to put out some bait, sweetheart," Fallo called. He and Henley were sitting on the guild hall roof. She couldn't decide what made her want to stab him more. The list was getting quite lengthy.

She didn't have any bait to put out, and she could hardly leave the roof she had just claimed to go scavenging for giblets. Feeling foolish, she slitted her eyes and pretended to nap. The mercus vision was still with her. The boys' haze of copper plugs showed quite brightly now that she knew to look for them. She breathed deeply and enjoyed a growing languor. The momentary nausea from her odd vision before had faded. It must have been the beer. Sometimes beer was cut with trezz. Kila didn't have much stomach for trezz, so even a small amount would induce visions. In Cheapsgate, the spicy liquor was everyone's favorite. It was cheap and its odd effects took people out of their misery for a while. She supposed Rammelstone cut his beer with it to make it go farther.

The odd heightening of her senses that came with the mercus vision wasn't so overwhelming now. She felt safe enough here, so she surrendered to it. If the obnoxious boys meant to attack her, they'd have done it already. The metal glow all around was pleasing. The tavern below her was alive with pewter, brass, and iron. A bit of steel here and there on patrons wearing swords or daggers.

Her eyes snapped open. The cat was there, standing over the empty dish. It looked at her with eerie green eyes. Its chin and breast were white, matching its white socks and the flag on the tip of its tail. The gray fur was short and smooth. It looked very soft. She wondered if the pelt would be of interest to a furrier. There was a very fine one—Danla Quire—in Gristenside. She dealt in mink and ermine and fox mostly. But surely one of the Radiant ladies would like to have some rare cat gloves to show off. The idea of selling off bits of the cat made Kila sit up. There might be more than two skillets to be had here. The skull and bones might bring some coin, too, if she could find the right ferneater. Such folks were always blending up concoctions to poison you or control your mind. And they always needed strange and rare ingredients. Unfortunately, the only person of that sort she knew was Finta Sahng. The Way of Til tended to kill ferneaters whenever they could. In truth, one did not want to know any true ferneaters. They might slip you something evil and make you their slave. That's what people said.

Kila's enthusiasm for parting out the cat waned. There wasn't much meat on the its bones anyway. You could sell a gull or a rat to a kitchen for a few plugs. That's what was in most chicken stews in Lower Terriside. But there were rats in the sewers bigger than this thing. She almost pitied it, for its ribs stood out as much as hers.

The green eyes were captivating. Probably because the beastie was possessed by demaynic spirits. Kila didn't care what Finta said about cats; the Way of Til wouldn't pay hard gold if cats weren't dangerous. It was axiomatic in Starside: *Take coin from a Donse Master and he'll own you in the exchange.*

She wished she'd made Henley give her his sack before forcing him off the roof. Even if she caught the little beast, she had no way to keep hold of it. She considered the ragged hem of her trousers. She might be able to rip off a strip or two to bind its feet. But even if it were tied up, she'd still have to carry it to the Cathedral. That was very close by. But going there was a problem because that Donse Master was after her.

She shivered. How had he tracked her to the Blasted Quarter? Maybe he had signed her bones when he'd caught her the first time. She rubbed her arms. People said that Donse Masters would sign your bones with mercus spells, and that way they could track you wherever you went.

"Why am I here?" she whispered to herself, suddenly angry. Hadn't she promised herself she wouldn't let anything lure her away from her task of getting coin tonight? She'd already seen how fast the cat was. She didn't have any chance of catching it, especially without bait. Or a net.

Wen would have thought this all through. He would have been prepared. And why did she care about a two gold skillet bounty anyway? She'd proved that pickpocketing was an easier way to get coin. Well, she'd almost proved it.

"Lovey, are ya gonna grab it or not?"

Fallo and Henley were still sitting on the guild hall roof, watching her as if attending a play at the Myton Theater. The cat was within arm's reach. It had crept toward her while she'd been repremanding herself. She lifted a hand, offering her knuckles, the way her father had taught her to greet dogs. The cat nosed her; its soft breath carressed her skin.

And then it pushed its face under palm and pressed forward. Kila was delighted by its softness, and its stupidity. She stroked the fur all the way down to the tail. The animal daintily stepped into her lap and pressed little white feet into her belly. It kneaded her with soft prods. A buzzing noise vibrated in its body. With great caution, Kila took hold of it, hugged it to her chest.

Curses and groans came from atop the guild hall roof. "Kil's eyes! That's not fair. It went right to her."

Kila smirked at the boys. They were disgusted beyond all reckoning. Henley yanked off his knit cap and flailed his knee with it. Fallo muttered under his breath, but Kila's mercus-aided hearing brought her every word. He was demanding to know what Henley had been doing all this time. This earned him a sharp elbow in the gut.

The cat settled into Kila's arms and began to lick one of its feet with a small, pink tongue. Delicate whiskers sprouted from snout and brow. The grooming went on and on. "Yer a dim candle, aren't ya?" she said to it.

She now had a problem. The cat seemed content to be held, but she didn't want to carry it loose where anyone might see it. She needed Henley's sack.

"Boys, I got a deal ta offer ya," she said, letting her tongue go easy with a bit of Cheaps-talk. "I'll give you a cut of the bounty if ya give me that sack."

"One skillet, five silver," Fallo called immediately. Henley grumbled that he would agree to no such terms, nor any terms less than the total surrender of the cat into his possession. He sure did speak like a merchant's son.

"One copper plug," Kila countered. Negotiations in Cheapsgate didn't often deal in actual coin, but the principles were the same. Both sides customarily started with insulting offers and proceeded to argue until someone got fed up and stormed off. Apparently Fallo knew this and decided to cut it short. "Henley's convinced me it'll be more fun to stand by and watch you lose the cat again. No sack."

Kila got to her feet. The cat dug needle-sharp claws into her forearm and was now a large burr attached to her flesh. "Ow! Not so hard."

The cat's ears flicked, but it didn't retract its claws. The boys laughed.

Kila educated them about their ancestors with a string of molten obscenities. This tirade faded mid-streak as that weird feeling of being watched pulled her head around. From where she stood she could see a just a sliver of the Sorrows. It curved a bit, then disappeared into the Harridan Gate. Nobody was looking at her. Nobody stood on the rooftops across the street.

No, the feeling was coming from downslope.

She absently stroked the cat's head and considered her options. None of them were good. But it was the two scoundrels now openly mocking her that decided her course. They could say whatever they wanted, and laugh their heads off for all she cared. Two gold skillets would be in her pocket by morning. "I wouldn't take that sack now if you gave it to me as a Winternight gift," she said. "Do us all a favor, Hen, and put it over Fallo's head."

Henley barked a laugh, but he caught himself and forced frown. "Don't call me Hen."

Fallo smirked and nodded appreciatively at Kila's insult, which choked her goat no end. What sort of scoundrel laughed when insulted? A lousy one was what sort.

She rearranged the clingy cat, tucking it close to her chest with one arm. She need at least one arm free for balance. She ran to the edge of the roof and jumped. She landed atop the guild hall with an inch or two of shingle behind her heel. The boys watched her, a glimmer of appreciation breaking through their recreational contempt. She put them out of her mind as she plotted her course. All she needed to do was keep out of view of the street and certain windows, make many long, dangerous leaps, and traverse several miles of the city while holding a wild animal that possessed very sharp claws.

The only way to safely claim the bounty was to have Wen do it. He wasn't wanted by the Watch or that Donse Master with the bone freezing mercus rod.

That meant carrying the little beastie all the way to Cheapsgate. But first she needed to stop by Finta's to collect Wen's medicine. That posed another problem. She didn't have the bounty yet. "Kil's eyes in a bucket!" she muttered. But there was nothing for it. She'd just have to stow the cat someplace, steal some coin, then hope she got to Finta's before the old woman went to bed.

The next two jumps were easy enough, and she was able to go along the rear of the buildings to stay masked from the Sorrows. But the next jump was going to be impossible without both arms free. She decided to stuff the cat under her shirt, then tuck in her shirt tails and carry it like a baby in the womb.

It did *not* want to be under her shirt. Her belly and ribs took several long stripes from its hind claws before Kila gave up on the idea. She could hardly blame the poor creature. After being stuffed into that sack, it probably hated the thought of being put into another one. The boys thought the whole act as hilarious as a mummers skit.

She had to put the cat down to get off the roof and onto the street. She was sure it would run off, but it followed her, bounding first onto a narrow fence, then to her shoulder. And there it stayed, affixed by its claws.

This freed up her hands and arms, which made for much freer movement. The boys followed, keeping well back. They occasionally burst into more rounds of disgusting laughter. She couldn't hear what was said, but she knew boys. Their minds were pits of depravity. They loved nothing more than to scandalize each other with increasingly foul jokes. Kila refused to acknowledge them.

She decided it best to skirt right alongside the Starside Wall. The road there ran straight downslope. Some creative official had named it Wallstreet. It was used mostly by drayage wagons pulled by teams of massive atlens or horses. It was ridiculously steep. Any wagon on the downhill route was dependent upon its brake lever to keep it from running out of control, which was not an uncommon occurrence. Kila and Wen often watched the slope hoping to see such mayhem and carnage. No luck so far.

The men piloting the wagons didn't have attention to spare her a second glance, and hopefully wouldn't take note of the animal on her shoulder. The slope was cold under Kila's bare feet. Everything this close to the Divide was always in shade, and now that night was falling it was chill enough to make her appreciate the warmth of the cat against her neck.

When she got close to Ranci Park she cut north again. The boys followed her, much more closely than she liked. They were not laughing anymore. She deemed it time to lose them for good. She didn't want them knowing where she stowed the cat while she went stalking for coin.

The sky was fully dark now, and dim lantern light was glowing in a few windows. Crisp stars presaged a chill night. That was a pain, because her marks would be more likely to bundle their greatcoats shut. She admonished herself not to think about it. *"Worry is tomorrow seeking comfort today."* Father's wisdom made it sound rather simpler than it was. She straightened and patted the cat's head. "Best if you not worry about tomorrow either, little gray. It won't be pleasant, but for your sake I hope it goes quick."

She climbed onto a roof, careful to be quiet. There were no toll pails close by and these residents were not accustomed to foot traffic above their heads. It took a few leaps and climbs to get far enough ahead of the startled boys to bend east and clamber over the marshalling yard wall where the waggoners kept their empty drayage crates and wagons. The crates were stacked along the Starside Wall. She poked around until she found a large one with a loose lid. The cat peered into it a moment and then jumped in of its own accord.

"That was easy." Kila dropped the lid. It was heavy enough the cat wouldn't be able to squeeze it open.

Kila oozed into shadows and watched the yard for any sign of Fallo and Henley. Satisfied she'd lost them, she made quick passage back to the Sorrows and found a perch overlooking the Cheaps Market. She didn't plan to stalk anyone down here. But she waited a quarter of an hour to make sure the boys hadn't tracked her. She wouldn't put it past Fallo to hang back and let her think she'd gotten away. He was smarter than he looked.

But neither of the boys appeared. She had her coppers from the pewter mug to drop into a couple toll pails. She had no interest in going into further toll-debt, though she knew none of the shopowners would know. *She* knew, and there was such a thing as honor. Well, maybe not. But there was such a thing as dignity.

Three coppers wouldn't get her far, so she set out on a longer route than usual. That was the story of the whole day, it seemed. Her stomach felt it too, even more than her legs. She was hungry. Starving. Father said that hunters did better when they were hungry. He said hunger made the senses keener. Kila wasn't so sure about that.

Besides, hunting was a dangerous way to think about her task. Much better to scavenge for easy takings. So it was back to stalking drunks, which was pretty much the same as robbing someone asleep.

She got to the roof of the Yinn Inn and crouched at the edge overlooking the Sorrows. This was her favorite perch. There were a number of taverns just around the bend that serviced the type of folks who carried spare coin. The street was deserted. Perfect.

In the years since Father's murder, she and Wen had learned which sort of men to rob and which type to leave alone. Older men were less spry, but more experienced. That made them good marks because they wouldn't let their pride cost them their lives. Young men would fight, which meant they had to be very drunk to be considered. There were lots of in-betweens, and Kila watched their gaits, their postures, looked for the slight swell on their hip that betrayed a dagger. She ignored men with swords entirely. Such were always looking for people to slice up.

She let three men pass who would have been good marks if they'd been drunker. A lone woman scurried along directly below Kila, clutching a bag to her belly. She was dressed very smart, with a hat one would expect amongst a Tilsday crowd.

Kila wished her mercus vision was upon her. She was desperate to know if the woman carried coin. A well-off lady was the best mark of them all. They were soft, easily frightened, and eager to give up a purse to end a confrontation. This particular woman was headed upslope, shoulders drawn in. Head swiveling toward every sidestreet. Kila had held the mercus vision so much recently she decided it was worth a try to bring it forth on purpose. Again she relaxed her eyes, sought to witness the city without naming anything.

To her delight, metal sprang into view, the air went crisp with the sound of footsteps, the caress of wind over rooftops, and the distant clang of rigging in on ships in the harbor. Kila kept pace with her new mark, leaping gaps and skirting around chimneys. She got a little way ahead and perched in black shadow. The woman wore a gold necklace and two silver bracelets. In her bag were a few small sparks of gold and silver. Coins. Lovely coins. At least four gold skillets.

Kila backed from the ledge and dashed to a nearby climb-down. The woman came to the mouth of her alley. Kila ran straight at her, put her shoulder into the woman's hip and lifted. Same thing she'd done to that Donse Master. The woman didn't have the chance to scream. The impact knocked the wind right out of her. Kila wrested the bag away and sprinted straight into the chest of an armsman.

He wrapped his arms around her and squeezed. Another man took the bag from her. The Donse Master was already helping the woman to her feet. "You did well, miss. Here, take the bag. Keep the coin."

"Kil-damned Tilsboy!" Kila grunted through gritted teeth. The woman had been bait, and Kila had been snared in the trap. The Donse Master removed his pale rod from its sheath and approached. Kila's limbs stopped moving.

"Put her down, armsman. Go tell the senior acolyte we have her. He'll wake the Hargothe."

When the man had gone, the Donse Master bent over Kila. His face was haggard, hair unkempt. Kila wanted nothing more than to gouge out his eyes. He absently tapped the rod against his lips. "Your mercus potential is remarkable, girl. Do you know how close you are? You hold it even now, yet you manifest nothing. But I suppose the heightened senses are valuable for a thief." He squatted down and pursed his lips. "I pity you. What awaits you will not be pleasant. I pray to Til it's brief. But I doubt it will be."

His eyes lifted. "I hear them coming. Listen to me now. I hold no grudge against you. As a Donse Master of Til it is my duty to offer counsel. When he lays his hand upon your head, do not resist. Give him everything and it will go easier for you. Resist and he will double your suffering."

Kila could move only her eyes. The armsmen came into view, bearing poles on their shoulders. Mounted between these was a curtained box. The feeling of being watched overwhelmed her. It came from inside those curtains. It was looking at her. Looking *in* her.

Yessss. I feel you, Kila Sigh.

She screamed. Or tried to. Her mouth would not open to let it out. An acolyte trotted near and conferred with the Donse Master. "Dunne Skyll, the Hargothe wishes the girl to be put in with him."

"Can't he wait until we return to the Abbey?"

"We do not question his orders."

"Very well. Armsman, pick her up."

Again Kila was hefted by one of the armored men. He cradled her. She looked up at his hard face, saw the stiff whiskers and curls of hairs poking out of his nose. Tired eyes. His rank odor wormed into her nose. The sedan chair was on the ground now. An acolyte was pulling back the curtain.

Yesss. You are magnificent.

Streetlight leaked through the parted curtain. Blankets covered a slight human form inside. A flutter of wind widened the opening. Light spilled across a skull-like face. It had no eyes. But it saw her. It looked into her.

Get out! she screamed in her mind. *Get out of me!*

A sepentine hiss came from of the sedan chair.

"Seer Hargothe!" whispered an acolyte. "What pains you?"

"It is nothing. Put her next to me." A skeletal hand lifted, long fingers testing the air like tongues.

The armsman brought her to the opening. He paused there, waiting for instruction. An acolyte moved about inside, arranging blankets and pillows. The smell of rotten fruit lifted from within. Kila put all her will into moving. Just a finger. Anything. The armsman knelt and shifted Kila to angle her head through the opening. If she went in, she knew she would never come out.

Let me go! she screamed in her mind.

The paralysis released. Her fury and panic exploded. She wriggled and snarled. Her hand caught the armsman's face, fingers probed into his squeezed-shut eyes. Legs kicking, she twisted and screamed. Beyond her own shrieks she heard the Hargothe's pig squeals of agony.

She fell, struck ground. Air whooshed from her lungs.

Another man was shouting. "Kill it! Kill it!"

"Come on, lovey." Hands gripped under her arms

and dragged. "Get on your feet. Do we have to do everything?"

It was Fallo. Kila didn't pause to study the chaos all around her. She was vaguely aware of the Donse Master writhing on the ground, his mercus rod rolling across the paving stones. Armsmen were scraping swords out of sheaths. Acolytes were motioning for everyone to be silent. The Hargothe keened in pain inside his curtained chair.

The alley opened before her and she threw herself into shadow. A faint gray shape darted ahead of her, low to the ground. The cat.

"Keep going, Sigh," said Henley, "they're coming."

The mercus vision didn't make the darkness bright, but she sensed the path before her. She leapt debris that made the boys stumble. The gray cat was leading her, pulling her. She felt almost dragged by its presence. It was the same feeling that had pulled her from the Blasted Quarter to the roof where she'd found Henley trying to catch the cat.

Are you doing this? she thought at the cat.

The pull grew stronger, and she dodged rubbish bins, leapt fences, and then dropped onto hands and knees to squeeze through a hole in a brick wall. She came out into an abandoned old brewery. She knew this place. Very close to the Blasted Quarter. The boys wormed their way in behind her. The cat stood there, looking back. Its green eyes were bright in the dim space. Broken windows let in a haze of mercus light from the street.

They were well away from the Sorrows here. The

boys had their hands on their knees, sucking in huge breaths. Kila listened for the distinctive jingle of armored men running toward their position, but the night was quiet.

"They stab you or anything?" Fallo asked. His face was hidden in shadow, but he sounded genuinely concerned.

"I don't think so." She checked her body, but there was no particular pain. Just exhaustion.

The cat let out an irritable mewl and stalked off.

"Don't let it get away," Henley said. "We've been chasing it all the way from that box you stuffed it in." He stumbled after it. A clanging of a metal pail resounded in the hollow space followed by soft curses. "Where'd it go?"

Kila didn't bother asking how they knew where she'd stashed the cat. All she cared about now was getting out of Starside and back to her den.

Fallo nudged her. "What did that Donse Master do to you? Did he . . . ?" He mad an uncomfortable shrug with one shoulder.

"No! It wasn't like that." But she didn't know that. Not truly. "He seemed to think I'm a merculyn or something. They were going to drag me off to the Abbey."

Henley came back into the light rubbing his hip. His knit cap was askew and a floof of ginger hair peeped out on one side. "It's in a hole back there. I can reach it but its claws are sharper than Kil's own teeth." He sucked the back of his hand.

Kila knew exactly where it was. She couldn't see it,

but she could point to it. She moved into the deeper shadows. The pail tripped her and clanged across the floor. She reiterated Henley's curses, adding a bit more salt to them. Her mercus vision had abandoned her. It didn't matter. She inched forward, hands outstretched until they encountered a brick wall. Crouching, she probed until she found the ragged edges of a busted iron pipe. Big enough to get her head stuck in.

"Come out," she called to the cat, voice resounding hollowly in the tube.

She sensed the boys standing well back. She wasn't sure why they had helped her, but her thiefly suspicions were alight. They were after the cat, after the bounty. Only Pol's grace had crossed their path with hers. She figured they had only helped her to put her in their debt. As if that would make her give up the cat. "Where's the sack?" she called over her shoulder.

"Hen lost it in the scuffle," Fallo said.

Next came a soft "oof" as Fallo got another elbow in the gut. Then: "Don't call me Hen. And I didn't *lose* it. I put it over that brute's helmet. It was your idea to save the girl. You're too smitten with her to listen to reason."

"Smitten! I think my standard is a bit higher than this scrawny thing. A face like mine will require considerably more loveliness in a mate to make my children even reasonably passable. Besides, she already turned me down. Now, as for your other ridiculous assertions. It was not my idea to save her. It was the cat's."

"Cats don't have ideas," Kila said. "They're simple as chickens."

"Well that chicken in the pipe jumped on the Donse Master and bit his hand, then crawled up his arm and scratched his face. Maybe it wasn't an idea. Maybe it simply attacks men of Til."

"They have every reason to," she said, absently. The cat was deeper in the pipe than before. The sense of being pulled was growing tighter. "This pipe must come out somewhere."

"Sewers, probably."

Kila found the brewery's rear exit. It came out into a shoulder-width alley nearly as dark as the inside the brewery. She couldn't see the pipe since her mercus vision had fallen away, but she felt pulled in one particular direction. She went that way, ignoring the boys' scuffling footsteps behind her. The pipe did not penetrate to the outside of the brewery. Fallo was probably right about it draining into the sewers.

Kila never went into the sewers this far upslope. Only at the grate by the Cherry Bottom Inn. Nobody went in up here. This was the domain of the thinnies, a strange people who demanded high tolls of tres-passers. They knew some ferneater lore, too, for they blew poisoned darts from wooden pipes. Entering the sewers this far upslope would be testing Pol's good humor, and the fickle goddess hadn't been in much of a smiling mood of late.

But there was no choice. The pull was too strong to refuse. This wasn't about collecting a bounty now. Not primarily, anyway. Kila had lost her appetite for coin.

She only wanted to hide and sleep and forget the whole day. But she couldn't turn away. The cat might as well have been yanking on a chain tied to her neck.

Kila had to go half a mile downslope before she spotted a grate big enough to squeeze through. She grabbed and hefted. It was rusted shut. She wrinkled her nose. "I've got to get down there."

Fallo and Henley swooped in, clawing the grate and straining to move it. Kila added her strength and it let go all at once, spilling them onto their backsides. The grate clanged so loudly, Kila was sure the Donse Master and his armsmen would hear it.

She didn't want to wait to find out. Rusty iron rungs led down to darkness. She went in quickly to overcome what little hesitation remained. If an unpleasant task had to be done, best to do it and put it in the past. The darkness hid the ankle-deep sludge running along the bottom. She knew it was mostly runoff from the streets, but that wasn't all it was. The smell brought her stomach to her mouth. Breathing into her sleeve she sloshed away from the ladder, letting the strange pull of the cat guide her.

She found it in an ajoining tunnel which stood well above the level of the flowage. She crawled in, feeling in the darkness until touching the soft fur of the animal's body. It meowed and made that strange buzzing noise.

"I suppose I have to thank you for scrapping with that Donse Master. Wish I could have put some stripes across his cheek myself." The cat leaned against her and accepted some scratches under its chin.

And then it was gone.

"Kil's eyes," she spat. "Where're you going?"

Out of the low tunnel and back into a big one. Kila heard the flow of water, but she couldn't see it. If the cat had jumped here, it was surely being carried downstream. But it wasn't. She could feel it just below her. She turned around, flopped onto her belly, and thrust her feet over the drop into the larger tunnel. She clung with her fingers as she lowering herself, toes reaching. They met dry wood. A platform.

She dropped the rest of the way onto a thinnie-built walkway. Not good. Not good at all.

Gray light beamed through a grate far down to her left. The water oozed in the blackness, raising a hollow slosh and sigh in the air. The air was cleaner smelling here, but not by much.

"Where'd she go?" Henley said. His voice was hollow in the distance. They'd lost track of her when she'd come into the cross tunnel. That suited Kila just fine. The cat was trotting away. Kila followed. She fingered the outlines of the coppers she had in her pocket. Thinnies didn't take coin, from what she'd heard. They wanted gifts, preferably daggers and swords or pots. And not junk items like the dagger she'd taken from the boys. She wished she had it with her now.

She kept low as she trailed the cat, though she doubted it mattered in the darkness. The boys were being too loud, calling for her in harsh whispers. Idiots. She would be much happier when she was rid of them. They had only saved her skin so that she could lure in the cat. They didn't care about her at all.

The mercus vision would be quite handy at the moment. She'd be able to see grates or ladders, and surely there were scraps of metal debris at the bottom of the sewer tunnel. But using the mercus vision worried her. She was starting to think that using it drew the Donse Master's eye. He'd said she was merculyn about to awaken.

A merculyn. Kil's teeth in a cup. Kila trusted merculyns less than she did ferneaters. At least the latter had to stick you with a dart or make you drink a tainted cup of trezz to do you in. Merculyns could charm you into doing things you didn't want to do. They could make light out of nothing. Some were able to even set candles alight. The mere thought of someone making fire out of nothing gave her the shivers.

The cat kept going, moving quickly and pulling Kila along. At least it was going downslope. The thinnies rarely bothered people near the outlet into Cheapsgate. Soon enough she was below the Cherry Bottom Inn. She knew this section of the sewers well enough. She came out next to a flowing deluge that spilled into the Sourwater Inlet. She dropped to a stone ledge, which led by jumps and leaps to the first rooftops of Cheapsgate. Kila felt instantly better once she was under the open sky. The stars were still crisp and bright. Best of all, there was no way that Donse Master and his armsmen would get at her here. Not without her seeing them coming.

People didn't traverse Cheapsgate through the maze of unmappable allies. They all walked the roofs, from shack to shack. There were no tall structures here, just a long downward sloping plane of ruffled tin, crate lids, and shipwreck salvage. The cat arrowed straight for the center of it all. Kila jogged to keep up, for now it was loping along, going fast. "Where're you going?" she called.

The cat circled wide around Dox Viller's compound. Some called him the King of Cheapsgate, but he was nothing more than a crime boss. Once past his three acre compound, Kila followed the cat to the other edge of Cheapgate, where a freight road connected the docks to the Cheaps. The cat leapt from the last roof and alighted gracefully onto the stone pavement. Without a backward glance it slipped onto the docks. Kila followed, curiosity pulling her as much as the inexplicable compulsion that came from the cat.

It finally stopped at the gangway of a two-masted trezzer. Kila knew the ship. *Scarlet Swan.* It was owned by the Keels. The boy she'd stolen the cat from was a Keel, one of five or six brothers. They all looked the same, pale as undershorts and mean as pikefish. The cat tested the air with its nose and whiskers, then looked back at Kila. *Wait.*

"Huh?"

The cat darted up the gangway and vanished.

Kila's mouth opened and closed. The sense of being pulled had vanished too.

Come. It's safe.

The voice was inside her head. The same thing the Hargothe had done to her.

Come! Hurry!

Again the compulsion took hold. Kila padded along the gangway. This was stupid. Father had lectured her a hundred times to never go aboard a ship without the captain's permission. Never ever ever. Yet here she was, bare feet on the deck planks. There was a little light coming from storm lanterns at the bow and stern, but otherwise the ship was dark. And quiet, save for the soft creaking of the rigging. She went forward until she came to an open hatch. The cat was down inside the aft hold.

Come! They need your help.

She squatted and peered into the darkness. Green eyes looked up at her. The white chin moved a little and a mournful mewl came up. Kila sat on the edge and dropped through. The hold was musty and wet smelling. Shadowy crates were stacked everywhere. The Keels imported trezz, so these must be empties. The ship was probably going to beat out of the harbor in the morning to make another run to Wantin or somesuch place.

The cat led her across the hold to a larger crate with a wire mesh front. A cage. A terrible animal stink wafted out and Kila fought a gag. She wished she had brought down one of the lanterns. If there were more cats here, Pol had truly had graced her with a smile.

Open it.

"Are you talking to me, little gray?"

No answer. Kila felt alongside the wire front. She

found a loop of rope holding it in place. It pulled free easily and the wire titled forward. Catching it, she laid it softly onto the deck. The smell took her breath away and it was all she could do not to retch. Covering her nose with her sleeve she reached into the dark space. Eyes lit up. All shaped like the gray cat's.

Four cats! Five in total. That would make ten gold skillets. Nearly as much as she had lost in Chance's Corner. One cat nosed forward, hissing. It cut off abruptly.

Ignore Oly, he hates everyone.

A cat could not talk into her mind. It simply could not.

But that horrible, skeletal man had done it. Maybe he'd loosed the works in her mind, driven her mad. But was she mad? She'd seen plenty of madness in Cheaspgaters. None of those poor souls ever thought their minds atilt. They didn't have enough sense to ask if they were mad.

She didn't have time to muse about her own sanity. Getting these valuable animals off the ship was the task. Casting about for a container, she was startled by two shapes huddled in the band of light coming through the open hatch. A flop of hair. A knit cap.

"Get out of here!" she hissed. "Kil's eyes, I swear I'll stab your guts."

"What is that smell?" Fallo whispered. "I know I said you needed a bath, but sweet Ori in Ecstacy, I think you'd best burn your clothes."

"It's not me, you hatchet faced scoundrel!" she spat. But what was the point in arguing with these boys? Like all of such creatures, Fallo and Henley were ornery, crude, and annoying. But they might be useful. "There are more cats in here."

"Oh ho! A trove of gold for the taking."

"Shut up, Fallo." Henley dropped through and came toward her. She tensed, ready to fight. He paused. "I'm not going to attack you. Look. We each take a cat or two. Collect the bounty. Fallo and I take half. You take the other half."

"Generous offer for someone who refused to sell me a burlap sack."

"I'm tired. I want to sleep. You can come back to our atlen barn. Eat as many eggs as you want. In the morning we'll all go the Cathedral together and rack these animals off for coin."

"I can tolerate those terms," Fallo said.

Now Kila was even more suspicious. "Why give me half?"

Henley sighed. "We're trying to skip the arguing. We are on a ship we were not invited on to. And I—I have history with the Keels. They would love nothing more than to catch me aboard. My death would be slow and quite public."

Pressure was building in her lower gut. She realized it was like the compulsion to follow the cat. It was coming from the cat.

Hurry! came the voice into her head.

Henley took her prolonged silence as agreement to the terms. He reached into the crate. "Got one. Got two. Looks like two more in here."

Fallo was next. One came readily, the other hissed.

"Oly hates everyone," Kila said. Then she heard herself. Maybe she *was* going mad. She had been sloshing through the sewers, following a cat she couldn't see . . .

A dull thunk sounded overhead. They all froze, eyes on the ceiling. "Someone's up there," Kila whispered. Henley nodded. Fallo was wrestling with a pale cat in one arm. It seemed intent on clawing his eyes out.

The little gray mewled. The creamy cat went still.

Kila inched to the edge of the spill of light coming into the hold from above. Relaxing her eyes, she let the names of things slip way. Everything she saw became merely shape, color, and texture. The fishy odor of the docks and the musty stink of the cargo hold lost names, too. It was a mix of sensation, nothing more. Same with the sound of footfalls and the clang of rigging.

Metal began to glow. Pins in the wheels of blocks in the rigging. Iron bands around the masts. Nails. Tools. A belt buckle and curved sword right above her head. Gold and silver jewlery on fingers and ears. The sailor paused a long time. He hocked phlegm and spat, shifted his weight from one foot to the next. Then he wandered off. She supposed he was on watch. Not very attentive.

The cats must have been a prize from some far off land. This was a Keel ship, so it made sense that the boy she'd robbed had gotten his cat from among these. But why a wealthy Keel would go to all that bother for two gold skillets was a bit puzzling.

Once the guard had moved well forward, Kila hefted two empty wooden trezz boxes to the hatch. The boys needed no instruction. They climbed up and were gone. The little gray cat bounded after them.

Come! And stop seeing. You'll draw his eye.

The cat's voice was small, but not childish. Insistent but not loud. Different from the horrid seer's, whose voice had rasped against her mind like fingernails on slate.

He sees you when you use it. An odd pressure came with the words and Kila's mercus vision vanished. *Come!*

She obeyed.

The three thieves crept back to the gangway and quickly ran up the docks. Kila had to call the boys to a stop, for they were running toward the Cheaps. It would be pure stupidity to try going through the gate carrying cats. The boys were so desperate to get back to their hidy hole they hadn't thought it through.

"Come back to the Warren," she said. "I need to check on my brother anyway. And we have to figure out how to get these beasts all the way up to the Cathedral without drawing notice.

"The Warren?" Fallo said skeptically. "Parlo Odok doesn't like me."

"He doesn't like anyone."

"He has special reason to not like me. His man Jocko has standing instructions to brain me on sight."

Why did boys have to make even the simplest thing difficult? She wasn't keen on showing them the secret way into her den, but there was no choice. They could no more carry cats through the Warren than they could through the Cheaps.

"Why can't we take them through the sewer?" Henley asked.

Kila rounded on him. "Listen, Hen. I'm not going back into the city tonight and neither are you."

"But we have atlen eggs to eat."

"Leave the cats in the Warren and you can go eat all the eggs you want. Go for a swim in the Sourwater for all I care. The cats stay with me or the deal is off. Got it, Hen?"

"My name is *Henley!* And maybe we'll just take our cats and go to the Cathedral now while its dark."

"Do you think you can outrun me."

"One of us could."

She folded her arms. "Fine. Which one of you wishes to die? Because you know the rules about bargains."

That statement had a much stronger effect on them than she expected. In truth, she wasn't planning to give chase. Wen needed her. And she was not going to sacrifice the two gold she had in the little gray cat chasing eight gold in these other cats that smelled like a chamber pot.

"We'll honor the deal," Fallo said. There was none of his usual humor in his voice. This flat inflection was odd coming from him. It was the voice of a boy's father coming out of his lips. In a way it reminded her of how Wen sounded when he quoted Father.

"Then come back to my den."

They looked at each other, shrugged. The little gray

cat was sitting at Kila's feet. Scooping it up, she put it on her shoulder and headed for home. The boys followed. They did not like the rooftop of the Warren, and they both balked at climbing down the nailed on boards to her secret entrance over the Sourwater. But when Kila went down with no fear, and a cat clinging to her shoulder, their pride took over.

11

THEY'RE THE ONES

Wen was awake. He was sitting up, back against the grimy wall of their den. His brow was damp, cheeks and eyes sunken. Kila felt his forehead. The fever had returned. Spatters of blood covered his chin and the front of his shirt. But he wasn't coughing now, which was a small mercy.

His eyes lifted, dull and distant. "Stinks."

The cats' odor filled their small compartment. Kila tore a flashtaper and lit the little fish oil lantern. She hoped the acrid smoke would overpower the smell. Henley pressed his knit cap across his nose and mouth. Fallo didn't seem bothered at all. He scanned the two sleeping pallets, the loose boards of the secret entrance, and the tattered scrap of rug covering the doorway. "I thought you'd have a more meager abode. I underestimated your skill as a thief."

She shot him a dark look, which produced an irritating grin. "Wen, this is Fallo and Henley. They are scoundrels. But we've found five cats. We'll take them for the bounty in the morning."

That endeavor would be a big problem now. Wen was in no condition for such a trek. And she didn't dare go herself. That left her trusting the boys with all five cats. They seemed to respect the bargain now, but how would they feel when they had ten gold skillets in their hands. And now seeing her brother so ill, they would know she couldn't spend much time chasing them them around Starside.

The little gray hopped from Kila's shoulder and nosed toward Wen. He looked at the cat. A smile curled one side of his mouth. "Where'd you find them?"

"Long story. You should sleep. The boys and I will get the bounty in the morning. At first light. Then I'll stop by Finta's and—Hey, get off him!"

The nasty cream-colored cat had stomped onto Wen's lap and claimed it by plopping down on its haunches. Its fur was matted in dark clumps. Wen pulled his arms up in alarm, but the cat sat primly and began to lick it is flank.

Oly is satisfied.

"What?" she said to the little gray. "How do you—?"

Behind her the boys were sliding down the walls to sit with their knees up. Henley had an orange cat in his arms. Fallo had a larger, black one. It had the same matting fur problem as Oly. Fallo scratched the top of his cat's head. "These little beasts are not smart, are they? Trusting as hounds. If they knew what was coming, they'd be out of here like their tails were on fire."

The fifth cat, a fuzzy splotched black and white, kept away from them all. It sat in the glow of the lantern, grooming itself with great vigor.

Yes. They're the ones. The little gray's comment came so loud and so forcefully in to her mind, Kila staggered.

At the same instant, all three boys sucked in deep lip quivering breaths. And that was all Kila noticed of their ordeals, for her eyes filled with a vision of herself as seen through the little gray's eyes. Her face was slack with shock, breath caught in her throat. A flush of warmth, like the sun on a summer day, pushed from her chest to her throat.

When it had faded and her vision returned to her own eyes, she was sitting cross legged, holding the cat to her chest. It purred contentedly. Tears trickled from her cheeks and onto its soft gray head.

"Did you feel that?" Fallo asked, jaw slack. He looked half drunk.

Henley bounced the back of his head against the wall and blew out a long breath. "These things can talk."

Kila looked into the gray cat's green eyes and discovered a sharp intelligence looking back. *I had to make sure of you all first,* the cat sent.

Sure of what? she thought back at it.

That you wouldn't harm us. At first you would, then you started to change. Then he *came into your mind.*

There could be no doubt who "he" was. The

eyeless, living corpse who had reached for her with those long fingers.

She looked to Wen. He was asleep, brow soft, breath steady. The cream cat was still busy licking itself. At this rate it would be a ten-day before it finished. Fallo was trying to help his cat be rid of some clumps, pinching them apart with his fingers. Henley's cat had shorter fur and didn't need as much grooming. The little gray was spotless.

"He says his name is Huff," Henley said, marveling.

"This one's Lop," Fallo said. "She's starving. And is making some very specific requests. Do either of you have a pork roast?"

"That one's Oly," Kila said, pointing to the cat on Wen's lap. "And this . . . this is Nax." The name was already there in her mind, as certain as her own.

They looked at the fifth cat. It paused in its grooming to look back, ears pert and forward. But they all knew the answer to the unspoken question. Kila gave voice to it, firmly. "No chance. No bounty. Not on a single one. Not ever."

12

TIL HAVE MERCY

The cell door swung open after an unknown time. An hour or a ten-day, Skyll only knew his mind was on the verge of madness when it happened. Not from the unforgiving dark, or the stink of his own waste, but from the bones of his cell mates. He had not bothered to count the skulls. He didn't need to know if there were five or six. But he couldn't forget that there were some small ones. Children had died in there.

There had always been rumors about the Hargothe's cellar. A dungeon, really. But without all the usual implements and machines of torture. Just a block of compartments, each big enough for a man to crouch in. Not quite long enough for him to stretch out. Skyll hadn't credited the rumors, considered them the fantasies of bored Donse Masters of low status. He'd been wrong.

An acolyte beckoned him to come out. The dim mercus light of the corridor might as well have been the naked sun for how it scalded Dunne Skyll's eyes. He didn't step out so much as tumble, shoulder striking the floor. The acolyte made no move to help him up.

The hallway was frigid, and Skyll was naked. "My robe! Give me something, man. Til have mercy."

"The Hargothe will judge if Til thinks you merit mercy. But first you must be cleansed. His nose is sensitive."

The acolyte walked off. Dunne Skyll wanted to pummel him. Wanted to strangle him. Had he any skill with certain forbidden feats of mercus, he would have burned the man to ash where he stood. All he could manage was to crawl. His aged hips screamed with the effort. On foot it would have been a dozen steps to go follow the man into the room. On all fours it took an eternity. Gasping, drooling, crying with every inch. Finally the acolyte tired of waiting and came for him. He did not help him to stand though. He simply took hold of Skyll's wrists and dragged him through the door and into an empty room. No furniture, just a steaming bucket in the center, handle of a bathing brush poking out.

The acolyte dumped the water onto Dunne Skyll's body, then set about scraping the bristles over Skyll's skin. Red scratches lifted in furrows. There was something more than water in the bucket. It burned like drinking spirits in open wounds.

More buckets arrived. His arms and legs were pulled straight and his front side scoured as if he were the floor itself. Never in his life had he suffered such agony, or such indignity. Rage boiled in his belly, but there it remained until he convulsed and threw up a trickle of phlegm.

He lay there half awake, unable to gather strength to sit up. Standing was a fantasy. When he had dried he was carried to a bed. Rough hands stuffed his arms into sleeves. The warmth of fresh robes did little to still his shivers. When he refused broth, he was held by two men as it was forced into his mouth. It was fishy and unsalted.

When his awareness next returned he was was kneeling in the crypt. The Hargothe's hand was resting atop his head. "There was a spark spirit on the street with Sigh," said the seer. "Why did you not tell me?"

"I hadn't seen it before," Skyll whispered. "Not until it was on me. Biting me."

"Why did such an insignificant creature attack you? I have handled many. They are fierce, but mostly they are afraid. None would attack you unless cornered."

"I do not know."

"I felt Sigh near the docks. She has since gone silent. Go. Sniff her out." The Hargothe struck Skyll's mind with mercus probes, ripping memories and thoughts from his brain. There were no word to describe the sensation, save "agony." It ended. Skyll shook with convulsions. When his body calmed, he found he could stand. In fact, he was invigorated.

"Thank you, Seer Hargothe."

The limp form under the blanket didn't move. The

empty eyesockets were pointed at the ceiling. The papery breaths told of life, but little more. Skyll bowed and backed away.

Did you like your compartment? the Hargothe whispered into his mind. *My cells are hospitable, no?*

Skyll paused in the door. The old man was lying there behind him. Weak, unprotected. It would be nothing to stave his head in. Skyll felt the strength in his arms to do it. The Hargothe had thrust him full of wakeful energy. It would be easy.

But he would not get one step toward the bed before the seer dropped him with his mind probes.

An acolyte motioned him to leave, frowning at his delay. Skyll stepped out and headed for the stairs. A faint voice penetrated his mind. *Fail, and it will be the only home you ever know.*

13

THROUGH THE BOND

When Kila woke the den was too bright. The lantern had burned out, but the planks of their secret entrance were not properly fitted, letting in far too much daylight. Gauging by the angle of the rays, it was nearing midday. A ball of warmth lay on her chest. Nax.

Fallo and Henley are bringing food, Nax sent.

How do you know?

I often know what Lop and Huff know. When they are not too far away.

Kila blinked and looked at the cobwebs in the rafters. That was a lot of information to absorb.

She sat up and rubbed her eyes. Indeed, both boys were gone, which explained the poor job someone had made of sealing their secret entrance. Wen was awake too. A pile of grimy fur lay next to him. Almost an entire cat's worth. Oly sat on his lap, looking annoyed. And naked. Wen must have used Cayne to cut out all the matted fur. "It'll grow back," she said to the ornery beast. It was something Wen had said to her many times when he'd cut her hair. She liked it long, but it got ragged and untidy with all her sneaking about. Father valued cleanliness, and Wen valued whatever Father had valued.

"They don't understand what we say to them," Wen said. "Only what we think to them."

"Is that true, Nax?"

The little gray's ears quirked, but the cat offered no answer. Not right away. But then she lifted her little head and looked at Oly. *Oly says that Wen wants me to tell you that you did well.*

It took less than a heartbeat for Kila to get the significance of what had just happened. She blew out her cheeks and laughed. "Hooo! I could"—she thumbed her chest—"and the cats could"—she wagged a finger between Nax and Oly—"and we could steal . . ." She whistled.

"Anything we want," Wen finished. He smiled all the way into his eyes. Still sunken, still dark, but livelier than she'd seen in an age. The bond with Oly hadn't healed him, but it had strengthened him. And with that strength returned his lovely, conniving mind. No one could think up a caper like Wen. Had he been well, they'd be recovery agents already.

Tell Oly to tell Wen that I didn't get any gold last night.

He knows that already.

Tell him!

Nax rolled onto her back and yawned. Nothing

happened. "Did you get my message from Oly?" she asked Wen.

There was a moment of silent communication between her brother and his cat. "No."

Nax?

I'm not your . . . But whatever Nax wasn't, Nax couldn't say. A distinct sensation of flicking tail came through the bond, a disconcerting feeling for a tailless human. Kila squirmed. *Stop that. Would you please relay my message?*

Why don't you make mouth noise and tell him?

Because I'm testing what you and your nasty brother can communicate.

A few moments later, Wen said, "I knew that already. But I feel better today. I think I could go outside if I had some food."

Footsteps made the roof planks creak above them, followed by arguing between Henley and Fallo. Apparently neither wished to climb down while carrying cat and food. In the end, Kila had to climb up and fetch a pot and climb down with it. For thieves, the pair didn't seem very agile.

The meal was scrambled atlen eggs. Apparently the boys lived in an atlen barn in Lower Terriside. It was full of layers, which gave them an endless supply. The eggs were huge and delicious, but the boys ate with the reluctance of those suffering from monotony. The eggs were cold, but well salted.

"Could use some bread," Fallo said, giving the last few spoonfuls to Lop. Kila looked around the small den, wondering why she felt like someone was missing. "Where's Startle?"

Nobody knew where the unbonded cat was.

Nax? Where's Startle?

That's not his name.

What is it, then? And is he safe?

What do you mean by safe?

Cats sure didn't like to give direct answers. *Did somebody steal him for the bounty?*

Nobody stole him. He's hunting.

Tell him he needs to stay hidden. Most people will try to capture him and take him for the bounty.

Startle is not stupid. He was in the same cage as the others.

Kila set aside a bit of her atlen egg for Startle. Lop ventured toward her bowl, but she gave her a stern snap of the fingers. Lop ignored her warning and crept closer. Nax let out an annoyed meow and Lop reluctantly went back to Fallo's lap.

"I've been thinking," Wen said into the silence that followed. Henley and Fallo looked to him with clear respect.

Wen was sitting up, hollow cheeks and eyes a bit less shadowed now. The food had done him good. "The cats can talk across some distance. Oly said it was difficult when you two were at the barn, but it wasn't impossible."

Fallo nudged Henley. "I told you he'd latch onto it."

Henley merely nodded.

"You two have been working the Sorrows," Wen continued. "Tell me what you can do."

Fallo shrugged. "I'm quite excellent at purse lift-ing. Henley can play-act the victim to good effect."

"Tell me more about that," Wen said.

"He approaches people and says he was robbed and beaten. His accent is sharp and quick, and he knows all the right names in the Upper Terriside neighborhoods. People give him a few silver."

"You know the same names and same neighbor-hoods," Wen said.

"But I have this face. Hen has that sweet innocent one."

"Don't call me Hen."

Kila folded her arms and did her best to look down her nose. "They're both bumblefooted and don't know the roofway. I watched them stalking the Keel boy. Fallo went on the street the whole way. If the mark hadn't been so drunk, he would have scared him off."

"You didn't hear a single footstep from me, Sigh," Fallo said, catterpillar brow bunching. "You saw me from a rooftop. That doesn't make me bumblefooted. You were the one who was knocked to the pavement by Hen."

Henley sighed heavily.

"We'll test your skills on Tilsday," Wen said. "I'll go up to Dunne Medow Plaza today and look around."

Kila and the boys all made the same quizzical face at the same time. The Plaza was through the Harridan Gate. That was dangerous territory for a Cheapsgater. Watch patrols for one. The Cathedral and Abbey occupied on entire side of the plaza, which meant the cats shouldn't go near it. And it also meant lots of Donse Masters and acoloytes would be about. Kila wasn't at all keen to be seen by them.

"We'll need better clothes," Fallo said. He was looking at Kila. "Leave that to us. We know a few greathouses where the laundry is sent out."

"You going out now?" Kila asked. "It's full daylight."

"The cats are stealthy like you wouldn't believe. And we put a rumor into a few ears this morning that the Cathedral is no longer paying. The fact that we have the cats with us is proof. After all, why wouldn't we rack them off and get the coin?"

The two gathered up their cats and squeezed out of the den. Kila looked at Wen, who was still smiling. "What are you cooking up?" she asked him. "The plaza is not a good place for us."

"Remember when Father taught us the Pickpocket Warning?"

Not only did Kila remember it, she had fantasized about trying the scheme for years. The idea was to post bulletins warning of pickpockets at the throat of bottlenecks. When people saw them, they patted their purse to make sure it was still there . . . which showed pickpockets just what they wanted to know.

"Ah, but we don't have the bulletins," she said.

"But I know where to get them. Somebody owes me a favor."

Lots of people owed Wen favors. But she'd never known him to collect before. She considered who would have such bulletins and realized there was a letterer off Sidle Street that Wen had helped during a downpour. She couldn't remember the name.

"I'll see to it," he said. "You should rest. I want you placed to watch people patting pockets."

She nodded appreciatively. "And I can tell the boys through the cats which marks to follow and exactly where their purses are stowed."

Wen nodded, smiling. "And I can override your poor judgment. This is not about taking the richest purse, but taking ones with the most chance of success."

"Nobody'll catch us. The boys may be brickfooted, but they're fast."

"I'm not talking about getting caught, sister. Success means not being see at all. Not by the mark, not by anyone else. No witnesses."

If there was a creed to Father's method of stealing, it had been that. No witnesses. Kila hadn't been so successful on that point of late. But Wen's authority to overrule her choices didn't rankle all that much. What did it matter? With the cats help coordinating their picks, they ought to bring home twenty, maybe fifty gold skillets in one morning of hustle.

She got up and bounced on her toes. "This is it, Wen. We're going to move out of this den and into Terriside. If those fool boys are any good, maybe they'll hire on in our agency. Think of how good we would be coordinating job after job with these cats."

Wen leaned his head back. The excitement was beginning to tire him. His color was good and his eyes were bright, but his cheeks were beginning to sink in and his breath went shallow. "I can think of nothing else."

Kila's own enthusiasm didn't wane so much as a cat's whisker. She lay back and counted coins in her mind. This was it. This was their way out of Cheapsgate.

14

A BIT SHAKY

From her position seated on the lip of the fountain, Kila finally grasped the beauty of Wen's scheme. Even though it had forced her from her warm blankets before sunrise. And even though it put her in the shadow of the Cathedral of Til and in close proximity to Donse Masters.

It was all about pinch points and jostling crowds.

Kila glanced at the bell tower, a square edifice jutting from the plaza off to her right. When it rang at the end of the Tilsday service, people would pour from the Cathedral's gigantic doors and scurry down the one hundred stone steps to the plaza. Most would turn toward the Harridan Gate somewhere behind Kila. Eight out of ten of those would be too poor to bother with.

A smaller cohort would go through the Trialti Arch, at the northwestern corner of the plaza. The arch formed a short tunnel leading to the rich neighborhoods of Gristenside. These were the high-nosed, powder-faced, velvet swaddled, dainty-footed, fripper-frapper men and women of the Radiancies. These people were the targets of Wen's plan. Ten out of ten of them were rich.

Kila blew on her hands and snuggled deeper into her wool cloak and wrapped the skirts of her dress around her legs. The stolen clothing made her skin all prickly, but she was thankful for it on this brisk autumn morning. And not only for the warmth. Even Wen barely recognized her in them, especially with her hair wrapped up in a scarf.

Plucked off a laundress's drying line, the maroon velvet dress was too loose in the bodice, baggy at the waist, and so long it dragged when Kila walked. The ill-fit suited Kila because it allowed her to wear her trousers and quilted shirt underneath. And it hid her bare feet, a dead giveaway that she was no Gristensider.

Her breath plumed with every exhalation. It was only mid-autumn, but unseasonably chill air had settled over Starside that morning. Being near the fountain helped. Its waters were heated by mercus feats to keep them from freezing. The same force kept alight the mercus lamps sitting atop poles at each corner of the plaza.

They'd go out soon. The sun had risen but was still blocked by Dunne Medow Cathedral. Jagged shadows of the cathedral's spires angled across the red brick pavement. The shade from of the central spire still covered the fountain where Kila sat.

She wanted to get moving. She sent to Nax, *Tell Oly to ask Wen how much longer?*

Nax didn't reply right away. The sticking point was Oly, of course. For one, he hated Kila. For two, neither he nor Nax had much sense of time. Therefore both thought it a pointless question.

Just tell me, she sent.

Wen thinks it won't be long, Nax sent. Wen had surely been more specific than that, but Oly—being the spiteful little tangleball he was—refused to share the details. Just because. Kila couldn't see him from where she sat, but she could picture the creamy beast flicking his nasty tail and thinking his hissy thoughts.

Nax was in position across the plaza atop a teahouse. The resident pigeons of the plaza had begun to stir and were now providing the cat with some much-needed entertainment.

Kila decided not to reward Oly with an insult, but she glared at the spot where he and Wen were hiding. She'd helped boost Wen into that statuary alcove in the side of the Cathedral, just where the Trialti Arch opened to the plaza. The statue had gone missing two years prior, leaving only a pair of stone feet and jagged ankle stumps. The alcove was deep and shadowed, allowing a boy and a cat to skulk there without drawing notice.

Fallo now lurked on the other side of the arch, sitting on an empty potato crate. He was trying to not to look too suspicious, a considerable challenge considering his villainous face. His rotund cat, Lop, would be hiding nearby. Probably under the crate, likely eating something.

There was a risk Fallo would be recognized, he'd warned. His father was Tarek PiTorro, a notable caravaner. Fallo had mentioned something about his father thinking he was dead.

Henley was positioned just inside the arch, his cat Huff hiding somewhere out of sight. He had out a beggar's box seeded with the three remaining copper plugs owned by the band. No Gristensider would drop so much as a moldy heel of bread in his box, but he'd be in perfect position to move on a mark. As a merchant's son, his face was also known, but his ginger hair moreso. He kept his knit cap pulled over his ears to hide it.

Kila's knees bounced with nervous excitement as she waited for the bells to ring. The bulletins Wen had gotten were in place, and her eye kept darting to them. Red letters stood out on tidily cut planks. BEWARE PICKPOCKETS. A little picture of a long-fingered hand snatching a purse accompanied the lettering. There were two bulletins, bracing the opening of the Trialti Arch. She couldn't read the small lines at the bottom from where she sat, but she grinned to think of what they said. POSTED BY THE WATCH AT THE ORDER OF HER ENLIGHTENED MAJESTY.

Surely the Tilsday service had to be over by now. How long could a Donse Master go on about the Theb, and Til's righteous rage, and the temptations of trezz, and of the shared sin of low tithing that endagered the souls of every citizen of Starside?

The clomp of boots brought her head around. A Watch patrol came through the Harridan Gate.

Wen says don't move, Nax sent.

She had no intention of moving. After all, she was a lady who simply had come out of the service early for fresh air lest she faint dead away. The Watch wouldn't question such a tale at all, if they spared her the slightest glance in the first place.

Which they didn't. She watched them tromp past. A double squad of six men, whipaxes bouncing on their shoulders. It would've been more impressive if they'd managed to keep their strides together. As it was, the axes bounced out of unison and the whole effect was rather humorous. The sargent walked to one side, paunchy and red of cheek and nose. They were likely headed up through Gristenside to the Westbunk where the Watch was based.

Which would take them right through the Trialti and past their signs. The sargent saw them at the very instant Kila realized the danger.

"What in Kil's twisted guts are these? Simons! Did you post these signs?"

"Nosir! I was with you all these hours on p'trol!"

"Your the Sign Officer aren't you?"

"I am, sir. These signs did not cross my desk for approval."

The sargent pooched out his lips. Kila noted two of the men surreptitiously patting their belts to be sure their purses were still on them.

There was nothing to be done, but—She stood up and waved to the sargent. "I'm so grateful you took our complaints seriously!" she called to him. He turned about, mustaches twitching. He took in her dress and head scarf and decided she was above his station. He made a little nod to her. "The Watch takes all complaints seriously."

He clearly didn't know what she was talking about. She pointed to the nearest sign. "I told my uncle, I said: 'Uncle Radiant, there's pickpockets working the Trialti. My friend Miss Tilly had her purse taken right out of her market bag. Three silver, gone like it were made of smoke. And Janell whatshername who maids up to Radiant Gilok's greathouse, she had a book stolen. And a—a—" Kila couldn't think of what else could be stolen. But the sargent was waving thick hands at her.

"We've heard all about these pickpockets. Why, just this morning we apprehended the whole lot of them. Never worry your pretty head, miss. They're all shackled in the Westbunk." He turned on his heels and waved at Simons. "Take 'em down before a Radiant sees."

And that was the end of that. Kila protested that she'd seen some villainous looking men just that morning, but when questioned realized she might get Fallo arrested. And so she watched helplessly as the signs were pulled down and carried off.

Wen says that's that, Nax sent. *We should get out of the plaza.*

The bells sounded, deep throated chimes that resonated in Kila's chest. As the last rings faded from the plaza, poor and rich alike began to spill out of the cathedral, dressed in their finest clothes. Their faces were flushed with relief, happy to be done with another two-hour haranguing by the bloviating Highest Chilow.

Kila chewed her tongue, furious at the sargent, and even more furious with herself for not being quicker of wit. Had she delayed him just half a minute, the crowd would have come down and he'd never want to be seen taking down signs that warned of pickpockets.

No, she sent. *Tell Wen we can still do this.*

Folk began to turn toward the Trialti Arch. The cathedral held thousands, and soon a throng was pressing toward Gristenside. The narrowing allowed no more than five abreast. It was a beautiful bottleneck. Beyond that, carriages queued, ready to pick up their masters and roll them upslope to their greathouses.

Wen's job, from inside his statuary niche, was to look out for patrols and to second guess Kila's choices. He couldn't come out now anyway or he'd be questioned.

Wen says you must go, Nax sent.

Kila's blood was already full of sparks of excitment. And no small amount of trepidation. This was it. The plan could still work.

Tell him . . . Tell him I can do the trick.

It was dangerous, especially this close to so many Donse Masters. But they couldn't all be after her, could they? And if Kila could spot just three or for good takes, she could drop the mercus vision and slip away.

He says you should go.

They had no gold. No silver. No medicine. And Kila had already begun thinking about where to setup shop. She would not leave here empty-handed. The scheme could still work. It would work *better* this way.

Tell Henly and Fallo to get back into place. We're doing this.

The plan now hinged on her mercus vision. Two Donse Masters came out with the crowd and took position at the top of the steps, shepards watching their flock. Kila didn't recognize them.

Letting out a breath, she allowed her vision to relax. She thought of it as exhaling with her eyes. It helped that she was nervous. Picking pockets was easy, especially in large crowds. But picking the pockets of Gristensiders carried much larger penalties than lifting coin from Terrisiders. One might be dragged off to the Westbunk forever, or one might lose a hand, or the Gristensider might decide to dispense with such formalities and thrust a blade into an inno- cent thief's heart.

Much to her relief, the mercus vision came over her easily. Glows began to overlay her vision, adding new colors to the Tilsday crowd. Some objects were tiny, just sparks, like the gold clasp on a necklace of beads, or the steel pin securing a badge on a military man's breast. One man's entire chest seemed to glow with the brass of innumerable medals pinned to his coat.

Kila snickered to herself. That was Commander LiTishke of the City Watch. She noted his purse glowed silver. A few specks of gold there, too. She would not go for those coins today, no matter how satisfying it would be to swipe them.

Nax sent, *Oly wants to know why you are so stubborn?*

Tell him not to get his tail in a tangle. I'm looking for marks.

Look faster. Kila wasn't sure if that was Oly's message or Nax's. Her bonded friend was nervous about her using her skill.

She scanned the crowd, looking for fat purses on easy marks.

It didn't take long. *Tell Wen there's man and lady skirting the southern wall of the archway. The man's purse is pathetic. His lady's bag is plump with silver. They're going to the market, I'd wager. She's wearing a black sable cloak and a hat that looks like a buzzard. Purse on her right hip under her cloak.*

She wondered how much of her message would make it through the cats to Wen. Hopefully enough for him to spot the mark and make a decision. The answer came swiftly. *Henley's on it. Oly wants to know when you're going to give us something good.*

Kila left the fountain ledge and slipped into the throng. Her eyes locked onto a good one.

Can Wen see me yet?

Oly says that Wen doesn't want to see you. He says that Wen says you look like a two-plug tart from Cheapgate in that get up.

Little bastard cat. Wen probably *had* said that last part, but out of humor. But there was no reason for Oly to be sharing it other than to irritate her. *Nax, tell Oly I mean to give him a good soak and scrub later.*

You wouldn't dare! Would you? If a cat could be scandalized, Nax was feeling it now. But there was something like amusement coming through the bond too, as though she'd love to see Oly get a good dunking.

Kila sent, *The man directly ahead of me is hauling no fewer than fifteen gold skillets in a purse inside his coat. Left side. It's a challenging grab, coat is fastened tight.*

Wen gave the man to Fallo.

Fallo claimed to have nimble fingers. Now he had a chance to prove his skill. Kila assumed he'd be noticed and probably arrested.

Tell Lop that Fallo better not return to the den with the Watch on his heels.

Oly wants to know if you have any other obvious instructions you would like to share?

I told you to tell Lop, not Oly.

What's the difference?

That was cat reasoning right there. Kila shook her head and continued searching.

Oly wants to know if you are resting or if you are just lazy.

I'm looking!

She wished Wen was well enough to make a take or two. He could have robbed any of these marks and they'd have thanked him for a job beautifully done. He seemed content to stand watch. He said that studying the operation would help him refine it for the future. That was well and good for him. Kila never had much luck with plans.

Tell Wen to look for a fat man with a very skinny lady

on his arm. He's got ten gold skillets in a pouch in his great-coat pocket. Right one. I'd wager his lady's got nothin' but an easy virtue.

Wen says they're no good. Henley has his first mark's purse and is ready for another go.

Tell Wen to look for a crow-haired girl with her red-cheeked mother. Both in ermine and matching hats. Mama has a purse with eight gold skillets and several mixed plugs. Daughter's wearing baubles and rings. Hard to pluck without notice.

Wen says we shouldn't get too greedy. No jewelry cuts today. He's sent Henley for the purse.

Kila had never considered herself greedy. As Father used to say, *"Whatever you do, do it with skill. There is no vocation that cannot be done artfully."* To steal too much from this crowd would be in poor taste.

He's here! Nax sent. Fear cut across the bond and dropped her into a crouch. She cast a glance back at the Cathedral. It was him, the Donse Master who had attacked her twice now. A file of armsmen was coming from the great doors behind him. He was standing at the top of the steps, eyes closed. Passersby were staring at her. She pretended to pick something from the pavement then stood, keeping her head down. *Stop using the mercus,* Nax ordered.

Her vision slipped away.

She burrowed into the crowd and headed into the Trialti Arch. Anything to get away from that horrid man. All thought of stealing was gone from her mind. *Did he see me?* she sent.

I don't think so. Wen wants to know what you're doing.

Tell him . . . But what could she say? She didn't want to burden him with her fears of Dunne Skyll and his men. But that wasn't entirely true. What she feared most was that he would forbid her to continue at all. And that would put an end to their dream of going legitimate. And it would cut off any hope of securing medicine for him. Kila didn't have any other skills, nothing she could exchange for sorely needed coin. She wasn't skilled enough mending things to take in such work. Was too filthy herself to get work doing laundry, and labor work went to men first, and there were plenty of them ready to wheel ash, collect rags, or cart kitchen leavings to the pigman.

She only knew how to steal. And she was here, right in amongst the throng of Gristensiders. She glanced at waists, looking for telltale purse bulges. Anything simple to grab among a crowd already pressed together in their haste to get home.

And there it was. And it was glorious.

A ceremonial blade belted on the outside a man's cloak. Blatantly showing off his wealth. Perhaps he hoped to be included in the annual Procession of Radiants marching up to the Citadel. That was the only time such ostentatious weapons were brought out into public by respectable lords. Kila decided that this man of poor taste needed to have his load lessened.

His black hair flopped over his brow and ears like a filthy mop, spilling onto the shoulders of his rich green wool greatcoat. A few gold plated medals adorned his chest. Big ones. Not military, though. Merchant Council. There was no way the Radiants would allow a merchant to walk in the Procession with them, regardless of his overstuffed coin vaults. So he was one of those Terriside merchant hoarders who imported necessities, charged Kil's bounty, and lived like a Radiant. Brass buttons down the front. She just knew he carried a rich purse, too, well concealed under his cloak somewhere. The blade was as long as Kila's forearm. Solid gold by the looks of it. It was worth hundreds of gold skillets.

Can Wen see the man in front of me?

The one in the green coat?

Yes. He's wearing a gold blade. Probably useless in a real fight.

Oly saw him. Wen can't see him yet.

That meant Oly was too far out in the alcove. *Tell that little skinsore to keep his hide hidden!*

The crowd shuffled forward like market sheep being funneled into a holding pen. Wen's alcove drew closer.

Kila twisted to look back at the cathedral, but there were too many people pressed in behind her. It was uncomfortable, but she preferred it to being grabbed by armsmen.

Where's that Donse Master now?

Standing by the fountain. Where you were before.

Oly's ears and nose popped out of the alcove ahead. He peered at Kila then drew back into the shadows. Kila resolved to dunk and scrub him regardless of what happened that day.

Oly says don't let anyone see you steal anything.

Does he think I'm an idiot? Don't answer that!

They passed the alcove. *Wen says do not make the take.*

Why?

That's Tarek PiTorro. Fallo's father.

"Oh." Kila twisted her lips, considering whether that mattered. In fact, wasn't it justice to rob the man who had wronged Fallo? The weapon would be easy for Scivn Natch to melt down and would answer all their troubles. Parlo Odok had somehow learned that two boys were staying in the den. He'd threatened to raise their rent if the two were ever spotted in the Warren again.

Kila reckoned that if Henley and Fallo were successful, the band would finish the day with thirty-five gold skillets. Enough to buy a year's worth of medicine for Wen and pay off Parlo Odok for a good long while too. But PiTorro's weapon would bring more. Much more. A shop on Sidle Street, a license as recovery agents, and a farewell to Odok and the Warren.

You're going to do it anyway, aren't you? Nax asked.

Yes I am.

Kila could creep almost silently; she could run the roofways faster and jump farther than the others. She could knock over a drunkard and take his purse like a man twice her size. But for some reason her fingers got a bit shaky when it came to plucking things through stealth alone. But this was such a simple grab. No strings to cut, no flaps to flip, just a quick grab and yank. What had happened in Chance's Corner would not happen here.

With a crowd pressing around her, there was higher risk of being noticed. And the pull would tug at PiTorro's belt. He would feel that.

Her father had often repeated the pocket-picker's axiom: *"To make a hard pull, make a hard push."*

I'm going ahead of him, she sent to Nax. *Tell Wen to talk me through it.*

Oly refuses to tell Wen anything until you stop.

Stupid flea rug. Fine. She didn't need Wen telling her how to steal anyway. *Oh, I didn't mean you, Naxie.*

I understood that. But Oly does not have fleas.

Kila grunted. Cats were quite literal.

No snide response was forthcoming from Oly. He sometimes went quiet when offended. She decided she should offend him more often.

Kila pushed past the green-coated man, making sure to press a hip into the blade as she did. It's just the crush of the throng, my lord. Get used to the contact.

"Excuse me," she called to the couple ahead of her, dropping all hint of Cheapsgate in her voice and putting on her Gristensider posh. "I got word my granny is ill. Please let me pass."

The woman wore a fur hat that was, miraculously, wider than her bottom. She turned to give Kila heavy-lidded stare. "There's nowhere for me to move, girl."

Kila squeezed left, putting herself in front of PiTorro. She went up on tiptoes, jumping to see over the throng. She looked back the way she'd come. The crowd behind was just as dense. Perfect.

"I'll just go the long way!" she huffed. She spun and

shouldered against the flow, again bumping PiTorro. This time her hand clamped the hilt of his blade. She leaned even harder into him, shoving him sideways. That was the hard push.

"Pardon, my lord," she said, smiling apologetically. "Some people are so rude." She glared at a portly man with a gray fringe of hair around a pale head. He returned her glare with a sour look.

PiTorro caught her elbow in one hand to steady her. "It's quite all right, miss. One simply must get to the bedside of one's sick granny. But stay with me and I'll have my carriage man drop you wherever you must go. My driver is just through the arch."

"Thank you, my lord, but it will be faster on foot." She dove forward, slipping free of his grasp and drawing the blade with her. It came out with no resistance. That was the hard pull.

With the prize already concealed under her cloak, she dodged through the press and found a stretch of clear pavement.

Donse Master is moving toward you, Nax sent.

Fighting the flow of the crowd drew hateful stares and more than few ungenerous curses. According to many, Kila was no lady at all! These people hadn't passed from the sight of the cathedral and already the sermon was forgotten. She muttered apo logies and vague comments about her ill granny. When she finally broke free, the Donse Master was walking straight for her. Armsmen flanked him left and right.

Kila tilted her face down and hugged her arms. *I'm not using the vision, Nax. Why is he coming at me?*

Maybe he can feel it in you.

Kila skirted away from the man, keeping close to the gallery of shops and eateries on the side of the plaza opposite the cathedral. She didn't look to see if the Donse Master followed. She went up on tiptoe again and waved, as if greeting a friend.

He stopped, Nax sent. *Wen says to keep walking.*

Wen? Why would he be telling her what to do? *Did you tell him about the Donse Master?*

No. But Oly knows. Wen says to make for the Harridan. He'll distract the Donse Master. Hurry.

There was nothing to do but obey. There were many more people going this way than through the Trialti, making for an easy crowd to get lost in.

Oly says don't draw attention to yourself.

Tell that furface that I've been doing this longer than he's been alive.

Oly says it all the sadder that you are so poor at it.

Is the Donse Master following me?

No. Wen is talking to him.

Meet me on the roofway, Naxie.

Kila walked confidently but casually toward the Harridan Gate. If PiTorro realized she'd stolen his blade, he'd be looking for her scarlet head scarf. She pulled it off and shook her hair free.

The Harridan Gate fed out of the plaza through a longer and wider tunnel than the Trialti Arch. She was again shuffling along with the Tilsday crowd. She kept her head down and passed into the dark and dank of the passageway. It smelled of urine and boiled cabbage.

A minute later, hearing no shouts of outrage behind her, Kila stepped onto the Street of Sorrows. The slums of Cheapsgate were visible from here only as a smear of black chimney smoke hanging over the distant sprawl of shacks. The smell of rotting fish and the nose burning ache of lower Terriside tanneries swirled toward her on winds now turned easterly.

Slipping down an alleyway, she found a way onto the rooftops. Nax joined her. They greeted each other with a quick scoop and nuzzle. But Nax sensed Kila's urgency to retreat, so she hopped down and slunk ahead. Kila would have to stay low, which meant some of the necessary jumps were out of the question. She'd have to descend and climb a few times. Doing so in her ridiculous dress and cloak would be riskier than stealing the dagger had been. She pulled them off.

But now the blade was out in the open. She cut a swath of fabric from the dress skirt and wrapped the dagger up. The rest of the dress she stuffed in a ragman's wagon behind the Yinn Inn.

Where are the boys? she sent.

Wen and Henley are coming. Fallo is roaming.

Wen would be cross with her for taking the blade. But he would forgive her when he saw the coin it fetched. She considered stopping at Scivn Natch's on Smith's Row, rack it off and be done with it. But no, he'd pay a mere fraction of its worth. This needed more consideration, and Wen would know what to do.

Cradling the bundled blade like a royal scepter, she headed downslope to Cheapsgate.

15

TO FEEL HER POWER

"She was right here," Dunne Skyll said to the captain of his armsmen squad. "How could you miss her?"

The man had a deep crease above his meaty nose. It pinched tighter as he frowned inside his helmet. "I never saw a Cheaspgater here. None of the men did. We'd have grabbed her."

Skyll turned his back on the man. Useless. They were all useless. Sigh had escaped them twice before. A slight girl of no more than sixteen. True, the second time she'd been aided by those boys. And that vicious cat. But that made no difference. Strong, well-trained men—soldiers, no less—should have managed her easily.

Had Skyll possessed any of the Hargothe's mind-probe skills, he might have succumbed to his anger and spiked into the captain's brain. To share with the man the very suffering Skyll himself was sure to endure for this failure.

He forced himself to loosen his jaw. The worst could still be averted. This morning's failure was not final. He would simply remain away from the Abbey until he had the girl. Simple as that.

"Are you sure she was here?" the captain asked.

Skyll didn't bother answering. Sigh's mercus aura was unmistakable. She had been filled with it, just here by this fountain. And then she'd gone into the throng passing through the Trialti. Pickpocketing, no doubt. Already the Watch had several reports of missing purses. And there had been a ruckus with Tarek PiTorro and his men too. A valuable dagger had been lifted right off PiTorro's belt. Dunne Skyll might have enjoyed the man's misfortune under other circumstances. The merchant was an uppity striver, scheming to be annointed Radiant. That would never happen, of course. Not even Starside's queen, vile witch that she was, would reward such reaching from a mere caravanner.

"Must have been several of them working together," the armsman captain said. He was growing uncomfortable with Skyll's silence. Good. And for once, he'd made a relevant observation. Sigh had not been working the Plaza alone. The young man who had stopped to ask Skyll questions about the Theb just now must have been part of her crew. A sickly boy with the stink of Cheaspgate on him. Surely he'd moved in to distract Skyll. How had he known to do it? Skyll hadn't seen him skulking about before.

"She must have been disguised," he said.

The captain waved down a Watch patrol and went

to confer with them. Skyll returned to the fountain and sat on the ledge. He sank into the mercusine, listening and feeling for his quarry. The splash of the fountain water behind him drowned some of the noises of the Tilsday bustle. As a Seeker he was weak compared to the Hargothe. But he was strong compared to most others in the Way of Til. How many burgeoning merculyns had he discovered during his tenure? A hundred? Two hundred? When children turned ten, they were required to come to the Cathedral. Skyll, or another of the Seekers, would place a hand on each child's head to feel out their potential. For every thousand he touched, perhaps five had a latent spark. Of a hundred with the spark, perhaps three would awaken fully to become merculyns. These were brought into the Way of Til for special training.

Except the girls, of course. They went to Pol or Ori, as was proper. If Skyll knew anything about the female race, it was their power to undermine the will of men. The Way of Til could not have such distractions in their ranks.

But Kila Sigh . . . He did not need to touch her head to feel her power. If he could draw within ten paces of her, he was sure he'd notice her mercusine aura. Hers was greater than the Hargothe's.

"Dunne Skyll, the Watch confirms that PiTorro was robbed of a valuable dagger. He suspects a young lady who pressed against him in the crowd. He said she wore a red scarf over her hair."

Skyll's eyes popped open. "Truly?" He recalled seeing such a woman pushing back through the press going through the Trialti. And then he knew: "It was Sigh."

The armsman smiled. "The rumor is that PiTorro's House Donse Master can sniff out the blade's location."

Skyll didn't approve of merchants having House Donse Masters. Were he Highest of Til, he would recall all such men to the Abbey for reassignment. But in this moment, the arrangement was advantageous. "Dunne Postin is assigned to PiTorro. Come, we will assist him in his search."

16

HARDBLADE

Kila imagined that foxes felt much as she did when she returned to her den. A sense of safety and ease came over her as she slid through the secret entrance. She lit the fish-oil lantern with a flashtaper (pulled from their store of thousands she and Wen had appropriated in a stroke of very good fortune a year ago) and opened the smoke hole in the wall. The thrill of the take had not left her, so she bounced on her toes and did a sailor's jig, leaping over Nax and swishing the ridiculous dagger about like a shadline blademaster.

We did it, Nax. We did it. From now on, it's beef and wine for both of us.

Nax huddled close to one wall to escape Kila's reckless prancing. *Where is it?*

Where's what?

The beef.

I don't have it yet. Kil's stones in a basket! We have to sell this bone chopper first.

Thumps on the roof told of someone coming by way of the secret entrance. She quickly wrapped up the blade and stuffed it among the rags of her pallet.

Wen and Henley arrived together, cats on their shoulders. Wen frowned a greeting to Kila and squatted next to the lantern, spreading his hands to receive its warmth. He let out a lung rattling cough and wiped red from his lips. Oly hopped down and made a show of turning his back to Kila, flicking his tail side to side.

Henley plopped onto the floor and pulled off his knit cap. A flare of red hair shot up from his scalp like petals of a shineflower. But aside from the surprised look his hair gave him, he had a comely face and gentle eyes. And a whole constellation of freckles. He smiled shyly at her.

"Well?" she said to him, "what's your take?"

"Buzzard Hat made me work for it." He happily plopped a silk purse on the floor in front of Kila. "She had the spirit of Til on her from the morning's sermon. Her husband is a tiresome windbag, too. And drunk as a first night sailor."

"Ya *talked* to them?"

Henley blinked rapidly and clasped his hands in front of his chest in mock innocence. "Oh Lady Buzzard, can you spare a silver plug for a starving orphan?"

He folded his arms across his puffed out chest, putting on a look very much like Fallo's self-satisfied manner. "I had her purse in less than a minute, but she took hold of my hand. I didn't want to snatch it away and run. That would make her suspicious."

"And what makes you think she's not suspicious and reporting your freckles to the Watch right now?"

"Because I kept telling her I didn't like the looks of another fellow nearby. 'Watch your purse, my lady. Yon shadelurker looks mighty suspicious.' When she discovered her purse was gone, she started screaming and pointing at the poor fool I'd singled out." He looked around. "Where's Fallo?"

"Did you ask Huff?" Kila guessed Fallo was at a tavern, squandering his take.

"I just did. Lop isn't saying anything. Fallo must have bribed her to keep silent. Probably took half a chicken to do it."

Kila snorted and turned back to the coin they did have. "What'd ya get from lady ermine and her daughter?"

He clamped his tongue in his teeth as he scrounged in a pocket. He pulled forth another purse, tossed it to her.

Kila dumped both of the purses out on the splintery floor planks. Eight gold, thirty-seven silver, eleven copper.

"Where's the rest?"

Henley shrugged. "Before I swiped that purse, Lady Buzzard had *given* me two gold skillets from it. I left 'em in her pocket. She was nice to me."

"Fallo should be back by now," Wen said, wheezing. He was lying with his back to the wall, face pale and sheened with sweat. "He's had plenty of time. Why can't he follow the simplest instructions?"

Where's Fallo? Kila sent to Nax.

Nax sent, *Lop refuses to answer.*

Kila decided to say nothing. Not for Fallo's sake, but for her brother's, who hopelessly believed in the boy. Fallo was all jokes and grins, but they could all see he was trouble-hearted over his father's betrayal.

"I bet he laughs when he sees this," she said, uncovering the stolen blade with a flourish. "Took it right off ol' Tarek PiTorro."

"Kil's handle!" Henley said. It was a wonderfully crude invocation of Despised God's name, reserved for moments of supreme fury or—as in this case— shock. Kila approved.

She hadn't inspected the blade when her mercus vision was with her, but she doubted there was much silver and copper in the alloy. A dagger like this was a show of wealth, nothing more. And that meant it was gold. Henley held out his hand. She reluctantly handed it over.

Wen shook his head, brows furrowed. "I wish you hadn't taken it. Very foolish."

Henley scrutinized the weapon with a discerning eye, tilting it this way and that, looking down the edge to gauge the craftsmanship. "The leather on the grip is worn," he said. "Someone has wielded this a lot."

Kila hadn't noticed. She also didn't care.

He lifted the weapon and made a few slashes in the air. "Well balanced."

"What would you know about it?" Kila said.

"I've handled plenty of blades."

Kila let it drop. Henley wasn't a very good liar, so it was clear he knew what he was talking about. Merchant's son. Probably had lessons.

"There are no nicks," he said, studying the edge. He promptly put the tip between his teeth. He made a face. "This can't be gold. Way too hard."

"Give me that." Kila snatched it away from the boy. "It *is* gold." It had to be. Irritated by Wen's lack of enthusiasm, she wrapped it up and stowed it back in her rag pile bedding. "Just think about how we can rack it off for coin, brother."

A thump came from the corridor outside the rug door. Fallo fell through.

"Dead drunk," Henley said, marveling. "How did he do that so fast?"

Lop is not near, Nax sent.

Wen crawled to Fallo. "I don't think he's drunk." He pushed Fallo over. The hideous boy was red-cheeked and panting, lips white. He struggled to sit up. After several false attempts he started to spit out his story. "Ran. Whole way. Chased. Yilo Chuff."

They all asked questions at once. Fallo merely flopped his arms out and fought for breath. He was a hale lad, and reasonably well fed on atlen eggs. Kila had never seen him this winded.

Wen asked the important question. "Did they see you come into the Warren?"

"Who's they?" Kila demanded. "You said you were stealthy."

Fallo shrugged. "I have to go back out and get Lop. She was too fat to keep up."

"Who was chasing you?" Wen said.

"Where's our coin?" Kila said.

Wen glared at her.

She glared back. "What? I told him fifteen gold skillets or he can sleep with his atlens."

Fallo waved his hand weakly. "She's right, Wen." He sat up and produced two purses. Kila snatched them and dumped out the contents.

While she counted, he talked. "To the point. My father always thought my brother, Deni, a more suitable heir. So he had me killed by hiring raiders to spear everyone in one of his own caravans. They even set fire to the wagons. An expensive loss. But I escaped through Pol's grace. She probably felt she owed me for sticking me with this face. The brute my father sent to lead the attack was Yilo Chuff, a man not noted for his conversational skills. He's more of a, uh, how do you say this politely—murderer. Can't mistake him. Bald as an atlen egg and built like a bull. Wears black gloves year round. If a buyer does not pay father promptly, Yilo Chuff extracts payment in ways that encourage other buyers to be a bit swifter remitting what's due." He chuckled blackly. "Yilo has apparently taken to attending Tilsday services. I would have expected Kil himself to dress in a bonnet and sing the 'Loo-Ra-Loo' than Chuff to getting pious."

"Maybe he was there to guard your father," Wen said, flashing an angry look at Kila.

"What?" she said. "I'm just counting coin." And a nice take it was. Fallo had brought back *twenty-seven* gold skillets and ten silver plugs. Wen's scheme had resulted in more coin than she'd ever seen in one pile.

"My father was there?" Fallo said.

"Show it to him, Kila," Wen said.

This was not turning out at all how she'd planned. This was supposed to be joyous. She had wanted to reveal the blade to Fallo with dramatic flare and a moment by moment recounting of her daring stunt. Instead she flung off the wrapping and clunked the blade onto the floorboard next to the coins. They tumbled out of the neat stacks she'd made.

Fallo's eyes narrowed, his black eyebrow scrunching evilly over his nose. "You *stole* my father's hardblade? Have you tossed your skillets into a chumbucket? This is an act of—of—of—war! It's—it's—it's—"

It wasn't often that Fallo was at a loss for words, and his reaction made Kila's gut go all watery. "But we'll, uh, melt it down. Or rack it off to somebody. Nothing to find then, eh?"

"Melt it down? *Melt* it down? Do you even hear the words tumbling out of your mouth? That blade is worth *thousands* of gold skillets, much more than its simple weight in gold. It's a hardblade. You think you can just hold it over your lantern flame and dribble it into a nice gold puddle?"

"Thousands?" Her syllables squeaked as her throat went tight. She coughed. "All the better. We know some people willing to trade in certain sorts of items, don't we, Wen?"

But Fallo was having none of it. Spluttering and going red, he snatched the weapon and cast about for something to cover it. Voice falling to a whisper he said. "We've got to get rid of this. Now!"

Wen's nose quirked, a sure sign of worry. "What is a hardblade?"

"It's been infused with demaynic strength," Fallo said. "Don't ask me how. Father traveled all over the world and met some strange folk. This blade can cut through timber as thick as my wrist in one blow, and not a scratch or dent or dulling of the edge as a consequence."

"A shadline weapon, do you think?" Henley reached for it eagerly, spilling an angry Huff from his lap.

Fallo slapped his hand away. "It's not a shadline blade. By Ori's blessed bosom, you're all dense as beach-coal bidgits. If my father was a shadline, our lovely thief-girl here would be a few innards short already. He's well practiced with a blade, though. And this one here has taken off a limb or two in its day." He paused and scratched the wisps of whiskers sprouting from his pocked chin. "I'll wager that's why Yilo was putting up such a chase. I thought he'd recognized me. Now I wonder if he just thought I was one who stole it. I bet that's it. He never got close enough to recognize me. A woman in a buzzard hat was pointing me out to him." This idea seemed to cheer him a bit. But not for long. "There's only one thing to do."

"And that is what?" Wen asked, sparing a quick glance at a red-faced Henley, who was trying not to choke on suppressed laughter.

"I'll throw it in the Sourwater," Fallo said.

"Kil's eyes you will!" Kila cried. "I'll be throwin' you in after. I stole that blade. It's mine."

"I thought everything we stole went into the pot," Henley said, still failing to stifle his laughter.

"Nobody's throwing anything or anyone anywhere," Wen said. "I need to think."

"Well, think quick," Fallo said. "That blade is like a beacon. Father has surely got ol' Dunne Postin feeling it out right now. Probably the only thing he's good for."

"That your father's House Donse Master?" Wen asked. Fallo nodded.

Kila did not like the sound of that. A Donse Master could mark objects—even people—using the mercus. Once marked, they could point to it, be it in another room or a thousand miles away. "We should take it to Critt Sanglo. He'll know what to do."

Fallo threw up his hands. "This isn't a pewter goblet you snatched from some Terriside house-mother. Critt will not thank you for showing it to him once word gets round my father's looking for it. Father knows how to hold grudges. He might be the best there ever was at it. Dunne Postin'll be able to follow it around wherever it goes."

Henley said, "Then let's throw it in the Sourwater and be done with it. We can toss it out the back door there." He pointed at the loose planks that covered their secret entrance.

"Yes!" Fallo reached for the blade.

Kila smacked his hand away. "Now whose a beach-coal bidget?" she said. "If they find it right below our den, we'll be the first ones they question."

"I'll take it up to the roof," Fallo said. "From there I can give it a good heave. They won't know who threw it in."

A thunder of boots sounded below, followed by cries of women and children. Glass shattered and a woman screamed. Rough voices barked questions.

"They're here!" Fallo wheezed.

"Everybody out," Wen ordered. "Kila, take the blade up. Throw it as far as you can, but try to get to the other end of the Warren first."

Kila dove for the coins strewn about the floor.

Boot-stomps sounded down the hall. PiTorro's men were already on their floor. More cries and curses. Henley and Fallo were climbing through the secret entrance. Huff clung to Henley's back, claws digging in deep.

"Forget the coin!" Wen said, coughing and pulling at Kila. "Get out." He shoved her toward the exit. Nax climbed onto her shoulder.

It was a bit awkward scaling the outside of the Warren, poisonous Sourwater glimmering below, while holding a stolen blade worth thousands of gold skillets. Kila clamped it in her teeth.

Henley and Fallo were bouncing with fearful energy. Fallo urged her to throw the blade. Kila held onto it and began a sprint. The roofline of the old warehouse was uneven, rising to strange peaks, and sinking in dips. But at the opposite side was a sort of built-up platform, the remains of a lookout tower.

Fallo ran behind her, hissing and urging her to throw it.

She climbed the platform and looked out over the Sourwater. With three spins, she built momentum. She imagined the blade arcing out over the water and splashing in, to sink into the dank, noxious depths forever. And with it their dreams.

She spun a fourth time, and a fifth, now slowing. After the eighth spin she stopped and stared at the weapon.

"Has Kil kissed your brain?" Fallo asked, looking up at her on the platform. "Give me it. I'll do it." Henley had wisely continued his run and was already off the Warren rooftop and skipping along Cheapsgate.

Kila squatted and peered down at Fallo. "If it's so valuable, won't your father pay a ransom for its return?"

"A ransom! A bloody *ransom?* Throw—it—in!"

Kila spotted Wen trotting along the roof, coming closer. Oly paced alongside him. Lop trailed in the distance. At least they'd all escaped. And knowing Wen, he'd replaced the planks so that no one would know they'd gone out that way. That meant they had time to think things through.

Fallo waved Wen over and began a curse-punctu-ated tirade about Kila's madness. Kila paid him no attention. She set the blade on the platform and crossed her legs. Nax crawled into her lap.

Here she had an item worth a wagonload of coin. That was good. But it was marked such that a Donse Master could track it. Not good. But the dagger was exactly the sort of thing a wealthy man would hire a recovery agent to recover. Good.

By the time Wen had ascended to lecture her, she had the whole plan figured out. And by plan, she meant a very general sketch of what they could do, less all the details.

Wen listened and nodded while Fallo grew apoplectic and stormed off with Lop. Finally, her brother smiled and patted her knee. "You are lucky to have me, you know that, sister?"

She grinned back. "I do, brother." Because Wen would take the seed of her idea and make it a real plan. And it would succeed, and they would make a fortune.

But first, she had to get this blade well away from the Warren. Wen handed her the scrap of skirt she'd had it wrapped in. The fact that he'd snatched it on the way out told her he'd had something similar in mind already. And that he'd known she wouldn't throw the blade away.

She bundled it up and started down from the roof. There were armed men milling about near the main entrance. Parlo Odok was shouting at them and rubbing the top of his head in frustration.

They never saw her. She left them behind, running fast toward the sewer that would return her to Starside. Wen was feeding the plan to Henley and Fallo through the cats. Kila suspected Henley was getting a much clearer picture of it from Huff than Fallo was from Lop. But she knew Fallo. Once he was confident his own skin wasn't at risk, he'd fall into line.

The ones taking the biggest risks would be her and Nax. As usual.

17

YOU WILL KNOW DEM-KISK

The tiny compartment was warm and rank. The stink of old onions drifted through the floorboards from the apartment below. Two nests of rags were arranged against the walls. A dented old fish oil lantern hung on a peg, glass chimney black with soot.

An armsmen held out a hand, cupping coins. "These were on the floor. Thieves, no doubt. The Warren master claims Sigh and her brother lived here once, but said they moved away in the summer. He's a notorious liar."

The mercus was vacant here. And unfortunately it did not leave a trail for Dunne Skyll to follow. Skyll knelt and drew his fingers over the rough floor. There was hair here. Not human. A bit of black, a bit of gray, a bit of rust. He was no expert on animals, but if the troupe of thieves had one cat, perhaps they had several.

His knees protested as he straightened. What did

the presence of cats portend? Surely there were no coincidences here. Sigh was the most powerful merculyn he'd ever felt. And she kept company with cats in a city supposedly bereft of such creatures. No wonder the Hargothe wished to possess her. He had instituted the bounty on cats, in pursuit of a legendary spirit called a felnithel. Skyll wouldn't have credited the existence of such entities hadn't the Hargothe been so convinced. They were supposedly demaynic spirits that possessed animals, and which could bond to humans and grant them . . . He didn't know what powers the felnithel could grant. Obviously they were cats in form only. But after ten years of bounties, and countless specimens brought to the Abbey, the Hargothe had not found a single felnithel.

"'You will know Dem-Kisk . . .'" He quoted softly, hardly concious of giving voice to his trepidatious thoughts. There was no mention of cats or felnithel in the old prophecy of Dem-Kisk. But the dire weight of the cryptic verses resonated mightily in this room. Dunne Skyll shivered.

"Donse Master?" the armsman asked, breaking Skyll's unfocused reverie.

"The coin you recovered will go to Til," he said, holding out his hand. The armsman seemed reluctant to give it up, but he had little choice. Knowing the armmen's loyalty was not out of piety, Skyll handed back four silver. "For the men when your shift is done. Beer, mind you. No trezz."

The man nodded a grudging thanks and pocketed the coin. He would certainly keep it all for himself, since none of his brothers were there to see this exchange.

"Let us return to Dunne Postin's carriage," Skyll said. "The thieves don't know the blade can be tracked. It will soon lead us to Sigh."

He swept out of the stuffy den and through the too-narrow passages of the Warren. He wished he knew feats to dispel the miasma of stink he had to penetrate to escape the slummy warehouse. The unwashed Cheapsgaters did nothing to be rid of their filth. These people warranted no pity, only contempt. To fall into this state was a sign of their inferiority. Til rightly frowned upon their wretched character. Cheapsgate should be put to the torch and let the survivors swim to sea. That the monarch witch allowed Cheapsgate to exist just outside the walls of her city was a condemnation of her character. Surely one of her power could scour the slums clean within a day. But she allowed it to remain. And that meant she condoned it. And for what purpose?

Having no answer for this, Skyll forced his attention back to the problem of finding Sigh. Dunne Postin was huddled in his carriage. Skyll offered him the deference merited by his age by riding with him. If the old man knew who Skyll answered to, he likely would have died of a heart seizure.

"The blade moves," Postin said. His face was pale. Enormous gray bags drooped under his eyes. Wisps of unkempt hair sprouted from his spotty scalp. "It blurs. It's in the city again, I fear."

Skyll thumped the roof of the carriage and it began

to roll alongside the Warren, wobbling as it bumped over the shacks the armsmen had knocked over to make way for the conveyance. The displaced Cheapsgaters shouted curses from the safety of nearby rooftops. Under other circumstances he would have sent his armsmen to capture them. Turn them over to the Watch for a night or two in the Westbunk jail cells. Tonight he could spare no time for it.

"The blade blurs," Postin said. His eyes were closed and he swayed with the movement of the carriage. "As long as it moves it will be impossible to recover."

"Perhaps you could impart to me the signature you placed on the blade," Skyll said. He had no idea if such a feat was possible. Postin shook his head. Skyll considered whether the Hargothe would punish Postin instead of him if their hunt ended in failure.

But he knew better. The Hargothe would punish them both.

18

YOU WAS A LAMB?

They had a few things in their favor. The first was that the Donse Master tracking the blade's movements was very old. Even in an atlen-drawn carriage and with PiTorro's armsmen clearing the way, he could only move so quickly and for so long. Fallo said Dunne Postin was easily tired out, especially when focusing his powers.

The next thing in their favor was Kila's insight combined with Wen's devious mind. They were going to hide the blade inside a greathouse where PiTorro would not dare to send his men uninvited. The lord who owned such an estate would think PiTorro mad for even suggesting that his prized dagger had found its way into his home.

Not just any greathouse, though. It had been Fallo, of course, who had suggested stashing the blade in a Radiant's house. The lad had gone quickly from calling them all Kil-kissin' simpletons to reveling in his father's misfortune. "The man tried to kill me!" he crowed. "This is the least of what he deserves."

The final advantage was the cats. Just as they'd help coordinate the thievery that morning, the communication they allowed would be essential for the caper to come.

But first they had to get the blade into a Radiant's greathouse, preferably one who already detested Tarek PiTorro. Fallo had several names in mind. Henley chimed in with several more. Radiant Gilok was first on Fallo's list, but that estate was nearly to the Citadel. Much too far of a trek, with too many Watch patrols to avoid. They needed someone further downslope, closer to the Baths of Ori.

They decided on Radiant Hiolly's greathouse after Henley reminded Fallo that their daughter, Elise, had recently been found murdered in Radiant Gilok's hedge maze. It was a very sordid affair that intrigued Kila to no end. The aging Radiant Hiolly and his wife had no other children and were far past the age to have another. This meant many, many, many people were pressing suits to inherit the title once the old couple croaked. First among these was Tarek PiTorro. Radiant Hiolly knew this, so he felt a special hostility toward the merchant.

Henley and Fallo met up with Kila atop the Yinn Inn and together they worked their way upslope. For now they simply needed to keep the blade moving around the city. Wen had taken a double dose of Finta's tincture, paid for with one of the three gold skillets Kila had manage to grab before dashing from the den. Wen's cough had receded, allowing him to lurk on the roofway and monitor the slow progress of Dunne Postin's carriage along the Sorrows.

Kila did not intend to plant the blade in the Hiolly's greathouse until after dark, so they had quite a day of it, running the roofway, keeping low like hounds escaped from their kennels. It was great fun.

The cats were not nearly as excited to be constantly on the move, and finally all of them joined Lop atop the teahouse overlooking Dunne Medow Plaza. They nestled in the sun there, dozing. As long as their humans didn't range too far afield, everyone could stay in contact easily enough . . . if certain cats could be persuaded to wake up and pass a message.

There were no other thieves or shady types on the roofway during daylight, so Kila didn't fear running into any. This meant that she could pass the blade off to Henley or Fallo and let them run a long loop around Terriside, confident they wouldn't lose it.

All the running worked up a huge hunger, and she was delighted when Fallo returned from one such excursion bearing a piping hot engerberry pie and a ewer of fresh goat's milk. They shoved gobs of pie into their mouths with their fingers and cleaned their paws like cats.

"This is a mouse-minded scheme," Fallo said cheerfully. "You do realize that, don't you?" He was grinning madly, which made his face look particularly demaynic. "But I love it. Oh, I do love it." He elbowed

Kila, who sat on the Yinn Inn's roof, feet dangling over a back alley. Henley had taken the hardblade and was running Fallo's loop the other way round. "Do you know how to get into a greathouse?" Fallo asked.

Kila hadn't given it any thought. She assumed she would jostle a window open and squeeze through.

"Kitchen door. Never locked," Fallo said sagely. "Go in there and you'll never even have to go into the house proper. The servants have their own corridors and dining room and whatnot belowstairs. Just find a footman's closet or somesuch and stuff the dagger in the back."

That was helpful, as far as it went. But putting the blade in a closet didn't seem like such a good idea. The second half of the plan was to recover the blade for PiTorro and extract a hefty fee. The whole idea was to finally be what she and Wen had always dreamt of being. Hide the blade where someone might stumble across it and the scheme would fail.

"Maybe I'll just wedge it in a chimney," she said. "Never go inside at all."

Fallo guffawed. "You just do that, Kila Sigh. I want to hear how that works out." He wouldn't say anything more on the topic, but Kila got the clear impression he was making fun of her. "Have you ever been inside one of these houses?" he asked.

Kila gave him a flat look. How many Cheapsgate girls were ever allowed into the lowliest Terriside tavern? None. On what occasion would she have gone into a Radiant's greathouse? "I've wanted to sneak into one for a long time, but Wen won't let me. He says it's too dangerous."

"He's letting you do it now. What's changed?"

"He sees beyond this heist. If we succeed in recovering the blade for your father, then we are recovery agents. Others will hire us."

"I like it better when you talk Cheaps-talk. You getting serious on me makes me nervous." Fallo plucked a stray pie crumb from his shirt and popped it into his mouth. "As for becoming recovery agents," Fallo continued, "I do recall my ol' papa used to hire such on occasion. I had the impression they were expensive thieves."

"No! Recovery agents restore items to their rightful owners. We find them, we return them, and we get paid. It's an honorable trade."

"Mmmhmm. Well then, I guess it's all very simple to determine that your client isn't lying to you about being the rightful owner."

Fallo was being obtuse on purpose. She decided to not to fall into his conversational trap. The boy loved nothing more than an argument. And he was good at it. By the end you'd find yourself all tongue-tangled and arguing his side on the debate.

"Remember, kitchen doors are always unlocked," he said as if he'd never left the topic. "Radiants call on their servants to do, or get, or cook something at all hours. Pol prick my nose if I wouldn't rather be a latrine digger than a Radiant's cook. So, mark me. Find the kitchen door and sneak in that way. There'll be all manner of cabinets and crannies to hide that blade in within the first five paces."

Henley returned from his loop, puffing, cheeks red. He was happy to do his part, but he derived no particular joy in victimizing Tarek PiTorro. "Is it time yet?" he asked, eyeing the sky. The day was waning, and Kila could tell he wanted to get on with the adventure. Not because he was particularly eager for the excitement, but because he wanted it over with.

"We can't venture into Gristenside until full dark," Kila said.

Nax, find out where Dunne Postin is.

The answer was a long time coming. Oly was reluctant to wake up enough to relay messages to and from Wen. Nax finally sent, *Postin just turned around near the Harridan Gate. Returning downslope toward you.*

Kila craned her neck to look up the switchbacks of the Street of Sorrows. Taking the dagger bundle from Henley, she set off on another downhill run. She loitered on the roof of the Cherry Bottom Inn until Postin's carriage had come all the way down to the Cheaps. At that point, she bolted uphill again. She grinned to herself, wagering it drove the old man mad. His troop of armsmen were tired, sour, and quite obviously losing faith in the Donse Master's ability. Perfect.

It was dark when she rejoined her friends on top of the Yinn Inn. Wen was there too, and together they continued upslope. With the cats spying over Dunne Medow Plaza, they knew just when the way was clear of patrols and Donse Masters. They hustled through, gathering the cats before sliding through the Trialti Arch to Gristenside.

The streets here were quiet, as folk tucked into their fine dinners. As the band of thieves crept past the Baths of Ori, Fallo made a lurid joke about a Sensual and her seventeen lovers. The punchline being: "And they found her the next morning on the roof." Kila didn't get it, but Wen snickered until he had a coughing fit. They halted until he recovered, huddling close to a stone wall. Ahead of them lay the Street of the Diadem, a continuation of the Sorrows, but with a much nicer name. There weren't many hiding places on the street aside from an occasional shrub. Kila felt very exposed.

There would be no running the rooftops here. The homes were too spread out and set off from the road by large park-like lawns. Each was surrounded by stone walls. Broken glass adorned the tops of these to discourage would-be wall jumpers. Fallo said it was to keep young lovers from attempting late-night trysts more than to keep thieves out.

Kila thought it a waste of glass. The walls were rough and provided numerous finger-grips and toeholds. And avoiding the glass spikes would be as simple as crunching them down a bit with a rock.

"Which one is the Hiolly greathouse?" she asked.

This produced a strange silence. Finally Wen poked Fallo's shoulder. "You don't know which one it is, do you?"

"It's dark. I need to see the houses. I'm sure I'll recognize it. There's a great fountain in front."

Because Gristenside was host to the very rich, the thieves had to contend with the downsides of luxury. There were more mercus lights, for instance, which stood atop poles every thirty paces. In Terriside, such lights were helpful in casting dark shadows in doorways, rooftops, and the mouths of alleys. Here they illuminated everything in glaring white light.

More Watch patrols, too. Kila heard one approaching before she saw it. The only advantage remaining was that, like the Street of Sorrows, the Diadem continued to switchback as it climbed the slope toward the Citadel. This meant that one could shortcut it via public stairs. And so she led them to the first stairwell and shooed them up. Unlike such stairs in Terriside, these were not hemmed in on either side by buildings, but were open to view from all directions.

She hoped that the Watch would see four people walking calmly up the steps, and that they'd be far enough away not to see little details like her lack of shoes, ragged clothes, and cat perched on shoulder.

The patrol consisted of three men, two carrying whipaxes on their shoulders. The limber shafts made the curved axe-heads bounce as they walked. When accompanied by the jingle and clank of armor, the whipaxes' motion became a weird sort of dance.

"Slow down," Fallo said as they climbed. "The Hiolly house is on that first stretch of the Diadem down there." Kila scanned the section of street that passed above them, tracing the higher switchback and continuing up until she spotted the next patrol. They were moving very quickly.

"We'll wait for the patrol below us to go into Dunne Medow Plaza, then we hotfoot it back down. You'd better find the Hiolly house before that next patrol comes round the bend."

The night was chilly, and a cold wind blew from the west, bringing with it the icy flavor of winter plucked from the tips of the Honor mountains. Fallo shivered and looked up at the peaks behind the Citadel, only visible as jagged shapes of blackness blotting out the stars. He patted something tucked in the waistband of his trousers. Kila didn't need the mercus vision to guess it was that rusty old dagger of his. She'd given it back to him that morning as a gesture of good will. She already regretted it.

She noted that Wen had Cayne strapped to his thigh, just as Father had worn it. She had PiTorro's golden hardblade, still wrapped in a scrap of that morning's dress skirt. That left Henley alone among them unarmed. What a wretched band of scoundrels they were.

The first patrol disappeared through the Trialti Arch. Kila and her friends descended back to the lowest section of the Diadem. Fallo took the lead, looking left and right as they past each greathouse gate. Most gates stood open, inviting.

A carriage barreled down the street, drawn by beautiful rust-colored atlens. The thieves moved aside. The carriage didn't slow as it clattered past them.

"I think this is it," Fallo said, peering down a gravel drive toward a palatial home that could house three Yinn Inns inside it. Mercus lights glowed from every window, and the faint tinkle of music drifted across the lawn. A line of carriages stood outside, drivers huddled together in gossip circles.

And old armsman stepped from his post at the gate. "Is the Radiant Peline expecting you?"

"Uh, nosir," Fallo said quickly. "I was just admiring the fine tuckpointing in the brickwork. Excellent craftsmanship, that. Top shelf." Turning away from the man, Fallo's eyes bulged and he motioned them to move along. The old armsman squinted after them a moment longer, then returned to his shack, muttering.

"I think that was the Peline greathouse," Fallo said.

"Ya think?" Kila said flatly.

"Do you remember which side of the road the Hiolly house is on?" Henley asked. "I seem to recall it on the right. "

"Yes. I do believe that is correct. There was a fountain."

"How do you know?" Wen asked, his voice tense.

"Father sometimes went to the Citadel. He supplied some things to the kitchens there. He would point out his enemies to me as the carriage took us up."

"You've been to the Citadel?" Henley asked, voice dark with envy. "Father never took me. Though to be honest, he rarely had occasion to go. The Keels provided all the trezz up there."

"This is a lovely night for a stroll and some chitchat," Kila said in overly sweet tones. "But perhaps you two should find us the Hiolly house so I can get to work."

The next house was the last on this section before the switchback. And it was, indeed, the Hiolly greathouse. Fallo was certain because, even though it lacked any fountain out front, the closed gate bore the Hiolly seal depicting a sprig of holly in a hawk's beak.

The windows were dark. Not even a hint that someone lived there.

"I think, perhaps, they've gone to the country," Henley said.

"Do you suppose?" Fallo said, thumbnail clamped between his teeth. "The Radiant has to be home for our ruse to work. My father will just barge in if the old man isn't around to refuse him."

"Where do the armsmen sleep?" Wen asked.

"There's usually a barracks somewhere on the grounds behind the house. Ten men at most. Likely getting a little into the gray years, most of them. They get discharged from Her Enlightened's army and find work as private guards."

The boys continued to speculate on things they new nothing about while Kila approached the wall. There were no broken bottle spikes here. The guard shack behind the gate stood empty as a skull.

Can you jump up? she sent to Nax.

In answer, the cat leapt from her shoulder to the top the wall.

Dark on the other side, Nax sent.

Good. Kila was up and over before her friends could start hissing questions about her sanity. The only way to find out if anyone was home to was to look.

It did not look promising. The drive was lined with mercus lights, but none were shining. At least the darkness it made it safe to cross the lawn. Once her eyes adjusted she was able to avoid tripping over raised flowerbeds and rock gardens well enough.

Remembering Fallo's advice about going through the kitchen door, she swung wide around the house. None of the front windows were lit. A bit early for bed, she thought, even for grayhairs like the Hiollys were purported to be.

Behind the house stood several more structures. A barn—probably for atlens—a squat carriage house, and a long two-story building that she guessed was the armsmen's barracks. She noted whale-oil light coming from windows there. Across a manicured park was a stone building atop a rise. It was dark and windowless. Surrounding it all was densely packed woods.

She made a wide circuit, chancing a quick peek inside the barracks. A dozen men sat to a Tilsday dinner. They looked like armsmen who had absolutely no notion of wielding weapons tonight. Good.

The back of the house was lit by two mercus lights. A set of windows to the south were lit from within. And a row of windows just at ground-level were lit up, too. At least the servants were home.

Wen says the Watch patrol is coming downslope toward them, Nax sent.

Tell them to come over the wall. There aren't any armsmen about.

Moments later, Nax sent, *They're in. Wen wants to know if you need help.*

Doing what? We can't all go inside.

A distant cough came to her ears. Wen. He hadn't exerted himself this much in a long time. And Finta's medicine might be wearing off. It was time to plant the blade and get out of there.

There were several doors along the back of the house. Which one led to the kitchen was anyone's guess. She decided to go to the north end, where there were fewer lights shining from basement windows. She peered in one to discover a girl lying on her bed, clothed in maid's livery, reading a book.

Stuffing down a wave of jealousy for the abject comfort and luxury the girl had settled into, Kila slipped to the next window. And the next. There were certainly plenty of servants inside.

Chicken! Nax sent, darting ahead.

Sure enough, the aroma of roasting chicken sent tempting tendrils into the autumn air. The pie Kila had enjoyed earlier was long gone. Her stomach rumbled.

This is must be the kitchen door, she sent to Nax. The smell was certainly stronger here. The moment had come. She was about to go from innocently sneaking around to brazenly entering a house to which she had not been invited. A distinction that had real consequences. Caught outside, it might be a week or two in the Westbunk. Caught inside . . . She might spend the rest of her life imprisoned.

A high window over the door glowed with the orange light of burning whale-oil. She touched the door latch and gave a slight tug.

Oly says Wen says to hurry, Nax sent.

The door was locked.

Tell Fallo he was wrong about the kitchen door. And tell Wen I need the lock-picking kit. He was as loath to let Kila carry father's tools as he was father's blade. That was because he knew she'd use them, which meant she'd go into a house. But now she had to wait for him to bring them. This was not at all how things were supposed to go.

Kila studied the kitchen yard while she waited. It had a low wall of its own that encompassed a large garden, now mostly put to bed for the season. A few stalks of kale, and a rambling squash vine remained. A toolshed stood against the rear wall. Most of the yard lay in shadow. Beyond it, the parklike estate contin-ued, blurring into the moonlit treetops and deep shadow underneath. A dog barked from beyond the barracks.

Don't worry, Nax. He's probably in a kennel.

The hairs on her arms prickled as Nax sent a wave of trepidation through the bond.

Wen is coming, Nax sent.

Her brother loped from the north side of the house and met her. "Which door?"

She pointed. "Let me do it."

Oly slunk close along the side of the house, his

creamy splotches glowing in the moonlight. He was not a subtle animal.

Wen handed Kila a small canvas roll. Father's lock-picking kit. "This is not going as smoothly as we had hoped," he said. "There are quite a few more carriages out on the Diadem now."

Kila unfastened the tie on the canvas roll. It unfurled on her palm. She was always delighted by the many little probes and hooks and wires Father had made during his time as locksmith. Wen had apprenticed as a locksmith for several years, so he was quite adept at the art of picking. Kila had an instinctive dislike for locked doors and lids. They were like an itch in need of a good scratch.

Selecting two thin steel probes she knelt by the door. "You go hide. And take that mangy possum of yours with you."

Wen stifled a rattling coughed into the crook of his elbow. He knew he was a danger to her and everyone else. Choking on the convulsions of his wretched lungs, he shuffled back the way he'd come.

Oly stayed.

Tell Oly to go with Wen, she sent to Nax.

Oly wants chicken. Me too.

Kila bent to her work. She slipped her probes into the barrel of the lock, feeling for the familiar shapes and contours of tumblers. She was not much aided by her trembling hands.

The dog barked again. Oly's ears perked and his eyes flashed toward the source of the noise. Nax crept close to him.

Oly demands you hurry up. He's not leaving without chicken. From her tone, it was clear that Nax had the same expectation.

I'm sure the kitchen-mistress will be eager to serve you a platter just as soon as we break into her kitchen.

Good.

I was joking.

So no chicken?

No!

And not just because they were unwelcome intruders, or reviled cats, but also because she couldn't get the Kil-damned lock open. The dog barked again. A second later Nax sent: *Fallo says a load of carriages is coming into the driveway.*

What?

The front gate is open and a line of carriages is coming in. Henley says the Radiant was at Tilsday dinner and has invited friends back.

"Kil's tears in a bucket!" she whispered. Frantic now, she jostled the lock. Her heart hammered and her vision began to swim a little. That was bad.

No, it was good!

There was no lock, no door, no probes, no cats, no delicious chicken. Just the unnamed world. She was instantly rewarded by a return of her mercus vision. She studied the gray glow of the lock and tumblers. The keyhole was nice and wide, set into a brass face plate. She guided her glowing steel pick to trip the first tumbler, held it with the second probe, then moved the first to trip the next. It was easy.

But then the lock mechanism moved by itself,

pinching one her picks. Someone was unlocking the door from inside. She jerked back. The lock gave a well-oiled click.

With an inelegant frog hop, she leapt away from the door, picks tinkling onto the stone stoop. The door swung out, concealing her where she had flattened against the wall. Nax huddled behind her, trembling.

But not Oly. He sat on the stoop, licking a paw. The light from inside cast a rectangle of gold over his creamy white body.

A rustle in the hedgerow behind Kila told of Nax's speedy retreat. Panic charged through the bond and it took all of Kila's will not to recklessly trail after her cat. She thought furiously at Oly: *What are you doing?*

But she didn't have a bond with Oly.

An elderly woman's voice trilled from the door. "What's this? A Beloved One!" A delighted yet weepy gasp. "Oh you poor dear!"

Oly looked up and mewled pathetically.

Kila's mouth fell open. *Nax, ask Oly what in Kil's accursed name he's doing?*

He says he's doing what you couldn't. Getting inside.

But he doesn't need to go in!

But there's chicken.

A gray-headed woman about four and a half feet tall came onto the stoop and scooped Oly into her arms. "You poor, poor little fuzzy-muffy. What happened to your fur? Blessed Ori, but you're wasting away!"

The woman retreated. The door swung shut behind her. Fortunately she hadn't noticed the picks on the stoop. And the lock did not snick into place. Pol frowns with one side of her mouth and smiles with the other.

Kila snatched up her picks and returned them to the canvas roll and stuffed it into a pocket. Still gripping the skirt-wrapped blade, she gave the door handle a gentle pull. She peeked into the kitchen foyer. Smells of roast chicken, and fresh baked bread, and hearty stew bubbled forth, making her stomach twist and growl.

The little entry foyer lay empty. The old woman was keeping up a constant patter about Oly's adorable qualities. ". . . just a tiny little baby is what you are. But that fur! What happened to you? Did a mean ol' sheepherder think you was a lamb?"

Kila squeezed into the foyer and gently shut the door. The heat inside was a remarkable contrast to the outdoor chill. A hallway led ahead, bending around the foot of a stairway climbing to the main floor. An opening to the right led to the kitchen proper. With her mercus vision Kila could see copper pots and pans hanging from hooks on one wall. The old lady was in there with Oly.

Are you somewhere safe? she sent to Nax.

Nowhere is safe.

Ask Oly what's going on in the kitchen.

He's having some cream in a dish. And a bit of nice chicken. Bring some out.

Ask Oly how many people are in there.

A pause. Kila was tempted to just make a break for the stairs. But she had no idea where she was going.

More than one, Nax sent. Cats didn't have much sense for numbers, four being the maximum they could conceive of. Even that was a challenge.

Tell Oly to make a racket. Draw attention away from the doorway so I can pass by.

A mournful mewling rose from the kitchen.

"Oh! The pitiful little starveling. He's so unaccustomed to food it pains his wee belly."

Another woman laughed and made baby talk at Oly. And then: "Mr. Flad will hand him to Dunne Ko'ak if he sees him. I could use two gold skillets m'self."

Old woman: "You'll find yourself scuttling coal for a ten-year if you peep a word about this darling to anyone. And Radiant Hiolly'll find he's eating cold soup if he harms a twig of hair on this pumpkin's noggin. But let's put him out of easy view just in case."

"I s'pose. He don't look evil to me, Mrs. Nanli. Just a sweet animal."

"There was cats galore when I was a lass. All gone now, except this sweet potato. Yes! You're a sweet little potato, aren't you?"

Oly says go, Nax sent.

Kila stepped past the door and pressed her back to the wall. She saw two women stooping over Oly. The cat was sprawled across the floor in a state of total relaxation with his chin over a saucer.

She tried to look everywhere at once for a safe place to stash the golden blade. She crept past the ascending stairs and into the corridor beyond.

Loads of people arriving, Nax sent. *Front entry. Wen says get out.* To emphasize this, Nax sent an image that momentarily filled Kila's vision. It showed the front entry, now all lit up with mercus lights. A column of seven carriages had pulled into the front drive. Another one was arriving.

Her vision returned and she stumbled, shouldering into a door under the stairs.

"It's Mr. Flad!" the young kitchen maid cried. "Hide him."

Oly mewled, followed by the a hard thunk of a cabinet slamming shut.

Kila opened the door she'd bumped into, discovered butler's pantry. She slipped in. No sooner had she shut the door than Mrs. Nanli's voice came from the corridor. "Nobody here."

Kila swallowed hard and pressed a hand to her chest. The mercus vision showed her the brass doorknob, trays of polished silver cutlery, goblets of every size, decanters, knives, and serving utensils. All silver. All right there in front of her.

Above her were more cabinets. She tugged one open and felt around inside. Folded cloth. Napkins, perhaps. She slid the bundled up dagger behind the stack, deep in the back. It would have to do.

Thunks sounded above her head. Someone walking upstairs. More thunks and scrapes as chairs were dragged around. Someone ran down the steps, ringing a bell. "Visitors! We have visitors. Tea and assortments if you please, Mrs. Nanli. Tea and assortments. Five minutes."

Within seconds, pots and pans clanged onto cook-tops. Kila could see the copper glow of the cookware moving about, right through the wall of her closet hiding spot.

Oly says he was stuffed into the dark. Wen says get him and come out now.

With the arrival of guests, more servants began to emerge from their rooms. The hall was soon swarming with movement. Kila could hear their footsteps, curses, and laughs. And she could see their clasps, hair pins, and buttons.

No doubt the butler himself would soon come, and she'd be discovered. She eyed the other cabinets in the pantry. She might fit in one of the lowers, but they had things inside that she'd have to move elsewhere. That would make a racket.

The kitchen door wasn't far. She could just dash through before anyone realized she didn't belong. But they'd most certainly see her and raise the alarm. And they'd know she'd been in the pantry. So they'd inspect it to see what she'd stolen. And find the dagger.

More footfalls overhead as servants began ascending the stairs to see to the guests. That thinned the traffic in the hallway considerably.

Tell Oly to wreak havoc. I'll sneak out the door and leave it open for him.

Nax replied only with sensations of terror. Dogs bayed in the distance.

Are the hounds loose?

Hunting me. Hunting Lop.

Kila had to get out. Now. The dagger and the whole caper didn't matter a lick if something happened to Nax. Scanning the hall with her mercus vision, she watched the last set of brass buttons go by. She opened the door and crept out.

There was bustle in the kitchen but not much talking. She risked a quick peep around the corner, just in time to see a footman bearing a tray and heading straight for her. Pol's grace smiled upon her, for he was looking at his burden rather than ahead. She pulled back, heard a noise behind her.

A door down the hall swung open, a black-booted foot emerged. Nowhere to go except up. She backed onto the stairs.

She had seconds before the footman would turn the corner. He had a tray. That meant he was heading upstairs. These stairs! Mouthing a string of frantic curses, she continued up to the landing. A glance showed her the next flight was empty. She continued up. There was a door here to the main level of the residence. No good. That's where all the guests were congregating.

The stairs were plain, sturdy. The rail was well-polished, but not ornate. This had to be a servants' stair. At the next landing she found two doors. Her vision showed brass sconces on walls behind both. But there was gold leaf behind the door to her right. The gold was arranged in squares and rectangles. Picture frames. Such luxury wouldn't be squandered for the servants benefit, which meant the other door lead to their rooms. A line of brass buttons was approaching from that direction. And the footman with the tray was about to reach the first landing below. He would see her if she lingered.

Decision made for her, she opened the door to the residence and stepped into a realm of absolute luxury.

19

THE WEALTH OF RADIANTS

"Dunne Postin?"

Nothing.

Skyll tried again: "Dunne Postin!"

The man snuffled, then his chin dipped to his chest and a garbled snore tore from his mouth.

Skyll blew out his cheeks and backed out of the carriage. "He's asleep," he told the old man's driver. "The hunt has taxed him greatly."

"I'll return him to the PiTorro greathouse."

"No no. Mustn't do that. Follow me to Appell's Inn on the Westreach. I'll arrange a room for him there."

The driver wasn't one to argue with a Donse Master, so he simply nodded. The PiTorro armsmen assigned to Postin were less enthusiastic. But their captain understood. Tarek PiTorro had made his expectations quite clear not an hour ago, when he'd come along on horseback and demanded to know why it was taking Postin so long to recover his dagger. His threats to all the men had not been subtle.

Skyll hated merchants like PiTorro. They accumulated the wealth of Radiants without cultivating the manners. They thought their coffers alone earned them the respect due actual lords.

And in this world, in these horrid times, it often did. Postin served at PiTorro's pleasure, in return for tithes of great weight. Bribes, by any other definition.

Skyll pitied Dunne Postin almost as much as he scorned him. In truth, Skyll was exhausted too; he could only imagine the toll the search took on a man of Postin's years. Since there was nothing to be done until Postin recovered, Dunne Skyll bade his own driver take him to the Westreach.

His own driver.

PiTorro had been incensed to find Skyll riding with Postin. The man had not been able to articulate a reason, save the assertion that Skyll was "using his carriage as his own personal hack." There had been more. Questions about how much more feed the atlens would require for pulling Skyll's weight. The wear on the leather of the carriage bench upon which Skyll sat.

"Merchants!" Skyll said to himself as they pulled into the courtyard in front of Appell's Inn. There was honor in a farmer selling his harvest at market, or in a tradesman building a barrel, or wagon, or cookpot. But these merchants were nothing but wagon drivers and ship pilots. They did nothing but move goods from one place to another.

Skyll oversaw Dunne Postin's removal to a comfortable bed, then retired to a room of his own. After a light meal, he went to bed. Sleep was long in coming despite the fatigue in limb and mind. Sinking into the mercusine, he searched and searched for Sigh's mercus, but he felt nothing. Not even Dunne Postin in the room next to his. Not the Hargothe, who slept no more than two miles away. Perhaps the Hargothe was right about him. Perhaps he was weak, and vain, and faithless.

A niggling thought thrust itself fully into his mind. Perhaps it was time to leave Starside.

20

THEY CAN ALWAYS GET YOU

Where are you? Nax sent.

Pure instinct had taken over Kila's mind and body. After a dizzying round of near discoveries and evasions, she found herself in a bedroom. It was dark, quiet. Empty.

Her mercus vision showed her metal everywhere, and it was starting to make her dizzy. Her instinct to remain absolutely silent warred with the rushing energy charging through her limbs. The result was an overflow of energy that made her chest heave.

Kila? Nax sent again.

I'm here. Are you safe?

Dogs everywhere. Sniffing.

Can they get you?

They can always get you.

Find Wen and the boys. They'll protect you.

Oly is still inside.

Kila worried about Oly the least. He had human

protectors in the kitchens. Nobody would grab him unless he was stupid enough to go out into the open.

Tell Wen that I'm coming—

An idea bloomed in her mind so perfectly bright that she giggled aloud. If she could find a place to hide . . .

From the looks of it, this bedroom wasn't in use. The bed was made, but the rest of the furniture was covered with white sheets. Chairs, a vanity, bureau, wardrobe. They looked like ghostly blobs in the dark. Even the chandelier had been wrapped up to keep the dust off. If anyone did venture in, she could retreat to that closet over there. It was the perfect hideout.

If she stayed, she wouldn't have to sneak back in. She remembered Fallo or Henley saying that the Hiolly's only child, Elise, had died recently. This was probably her room. All Kila needed to do was stay quiet and wait. Wen could approach PiTorro with the proposal to recover his blade, and Nax would tell her when it was time to bring the blade out.

Tell Wen I'm going to stay here until it's time to bring the blade out for PiTorro.

You can't stay, Nax sent. *Dogs!*

The dogs are outside. I'm inside. Go with Wen. Get away.

Oly hates your plan. Oly says you are stupid.

Kila had a hunch that Nax was putting words into Oly's mind. Oly would have been much more insulting than that.

Tell Oly to stay quiet. Think of all the chicken and cream he'll get.

Oly won't tell Wen anything. He hates your plan.

Then tell Lop and Huff.

Resistance came through the bond, like the feeling of stiffening one's limbs to keep from being stuffed into a box. *Huff says Henley says Wen says it's not a bad plan. Fallo thinks it will be a—a—* Confusion and discomfort prickled Kila's skin as Nax struggled with a concept alien to a cat's mind. A *ten-day?* she finished.

Why so long?

Fallo is saying many things. Lop is making it shorter. His father will wait to see if his Donse Master can find the blade. Maybe not a ten-day. Fallo talks a lot. Lop isn't paying attention anymore.

Kila was beginning to feel a bit queasy. The mercus vision had not let up and her heightened senses were overwhelming her. The dust of the stuffy bedroom stank of mildew. Her own heartbeat thundered. From downstairs she heard tinkles of glass, occasional bawdy laughs, and innumerable footsteps. Radiants really did up Tilsday like it was Winternight. She wondered how much coin they frittered away on parties like this. Probably enough to feed half of Cheapsgate for a week. She uncovered an armchair and plopped into it, legs crossed. She focused more on her breathing, working to slow her heart and release the mercus vision.

She had no doubt she could get it back under these circumstances. A warm feeling came over her as she let her mind drift. Footsteps sounded in the hall, but no one was going to come in here.

A cold splash sent her bolt upright, slithering

down her spine like drips of ice water. That horrid feeling of being watched. She forced herself to relax. Breathing out, she let go. The mercus vision faded and the world dimmed. The slithery feeling vanished, but her pulse slammed in her ears.

The dogs went away, Nax sent. *I found Wen. He is talking to me with his mouth.*

Can you understand what he's saying?

No. Huff says Henley says Wen asks if you are somewhere safe.

Yes.

We are going over the wall.

Goodbye, Naxie. I'll see you soon.

No answer except irritation.

Shortly after, she felt the cat fading. Once Nax was beyond Dunne Medow Plaza, she knew they would not be able to communicate at all. She didn't like that. But with the mercus vision gone and her senses duly muted, she became sleepy. Just to be safe, she moved into the closet. She found an enormous array of gowns. These had belonged to Elise Hiolly, who had apparently been fully grown when murdered.

Kila collected a few of the softest dresses and made a nest on the floor. She would just nap for a while. Then, when the house was quiet, she would slip out and see what she might see.

21

WINTER DID NOT OBEY

A change in the house woke Kila. Nothing startling, just a quietening sensation. A restfulness in contrast to the noise of the party. The Warren sometimes experienced sudden lulls like this when folks decided to go to sleep.

Kila peeked out. The hallway was empty but brightly lit. Narrow sidetables held sprays of flowers and other ornamental pieces. The Hiollys had a preference for a glossy black urns, all rimmed with gold. Paintings of long-dead Hiolly forebears stared sternly from their frames. Each was lit with a little mercus light so that their dour faces could be seen at all hours.

Thick carpet ran the length of the hallway. It was piled so thickly a pony could have walked silently on it. Probably made in Trine or some other far-flung realm. Every five paces the Hiolly crest was woven in gold. Each bedroom door was set into a little alcove, giving her a bit of cover in case someone came out of the . . . five, six, seven bedrooms. Seven! And there was an entire south wing, and a third floor above.

She headed back toward the servants' stair, but a sudden noise sent her scrambling into next room. This one was empty, but the furniture had not been covered. A guest room, perhaps. There were no personal items in view.

She crept to the window and peered out over the front lawn. A gentleman and lady were boarding a carriage. And there were several more people coming down the front steps. The little gala was indeed breaking up. Perhaps the elderly Hiolly's were determined to have an early night.

This was both good and bad. Once everyone cleared out, things belowstairs would settle down quickly. She'd be able to sneak down and collect the blade. In the meantime she felt secure enough upstairs to poke her nose into a few more rooms. She listened at the door directly across the hall but heard nothing. It wasn't locked. She crept in.

"Put the tray on the table, Lilli," a man said.

Kila stopped mid-step, eyes darting to the bed from which the voice had come. Another softer voice rose too, forming the syllables of sensual pleasure. An amorphous, writhing bulge moved beneath the blankets, which sprouted two heads. Cheeks burning, Kila backed from the room. Obviously not the Radiant and his wife. And their only child was dead, so not Elise. That meant these were overnight guests. That particular couple must have found the entertainments downstairs less interesting than the ones they could devise for themselves.

Kila was no prude, but . . . Well, maybe she was a bit of a prude. Neither of the lovers had seen her. They had assumed she was a servant come with a tray. Which meant they had summoned a servant. Which meant—

The servants' door at the end of the hall opened. Kila dove into the cover of the alcove opposite the lovers' room. With shaky hands she opened the door and eased through, cringing at the slight squeak of the hinges.

"Someone there?" called the maid. Lilli, Kila presumed. "Helloooo!"

Kila's mercus vision arose unbidden. Through the door, she saw the maid's silver platter floating at waist-height.

"Hellooo?" Lilli called in a frightened squeak. "Elise? Is that—is that—you?"

The man barked irritably from the other bedroom. The maid went in with the tray. Kila leaned her back to the wall and sucked air. The man berated the maid for coming and going. The girl took it in stride and offered no explanation or excuses. Kila couldn't understand why the couple would allow anyone in while they were engaged in what the Theb called Til's Mandate.

She listened for their door to close and the maid to retreat belowstairs. She needed to remember that people did not always wear metal, especially if they were wearing nothing at all. She waited until the mercus vision retreated, offering prayers to Kil and Til and all the rest, she hadn't held it long enough to attract the attention of any Donse Masters.

Proceeding with more caution, she sneaked into the hall, determined to return to Elise's room and wait patiently until she was sure everyone had gone to bed. Trouble was, she was bored. She needed a distraction. A book. She liked reading, though she had little enough opportunity. Cheapsgate wasn't known for its libraries. Father had valued reading above all else, had taught her from a copy of the Theb. He'd even taught her a few phrases of the First Race tongue.

Elise had not been a reader, it seemed. But surely one of these rooms had books in it.

No. She needed to hide and stay hidden. She would simply have to entertain herself by reviewing her life to come on Curling Street, or Sidle, or somewhere nearer to Upper Terriside. And so she did, for a quarter of an hour before she again grew antsy. So she paced and looked out the window onto the back lawn. The kitchen garden was just below. She wanted to see out to the front and see how many carriages remained.

She decided to risk a little dash across the hall to a room she knew to be empty. Her hand was on the knob when she heard a low voice inside. Another guest had decided to overnight in the Hiolly greathouse.

Slipping past the top of a wide stairs overlooking the entry foyer, she went to the next door. It was tempting to bring the mercus vision forth, but she dared not. She pressed her ear to the door. Nothing.

The door was different from the others, for it was a set of two, hinged on opposite sides. She opened one and peered in. A library! A true library. Kila had never seen so many books in one place. A shaggy creature slept on the floor. To Kila's startled brain it looked like a white wolf, with bull shoulders, and a long snout. It slept near the fireplace. This was the Radiant's study. The hound likely his fondest friend.

A bit of Kila's aroma reached it. Nostrils snuffling, it cracked an eye and looked to the door. The massive head slowly lifted, a deep-throated rumble rolling from its throat. Lips curled up to reveal its meat-rippers.

Air whipped past Kila's face as she sprinted down the hall. Barks and howls sounded behind her. Her bare feet skittered and slid as she turned into Elise's room.

The dog barked and pounded down the hall. Voices rose in the house, calling for Winter to be still. But ol' Winter would not be still. She posted herself at Kila's door, barking and growling and pawing.

Kila was sure she'd gotten inside before it had come out of the study, but somehow it knew where she'd gone. Smacking her forehead, she cursed her stupidity. It was a hound. It could smell her. Already people were stomping up the steps to see what had gotten Winter into such a frenzy.

They would search the room.

Her eyes went to the window behind her. The brass latch glowed. The mercus vision had snapped to the fore once again.

People called for Winter to be quiet. Winter did not obey.

The latch released at Kila's touch. She swung the window out. Cool air whipped in. Hedges and cobblestones lay far below. There was a slight ledge below the window, little more than a decorative band of brick. No hesitation now. Kila went through, toes finding and holding the ledge. Window shut. No way to latch it. Winter howling. People shouting.

Finger holds. A rain gutter. Up. Easy as climbing to the roofway. Breath heaving and heart in her throat, Kila peered over the eve of the third story dormer. A servant's head popped from the window she'd come through. He craned to look this way and that. He never thought to look up. Finally he withdrew. With quick steps and leaps, Kila gained the ridge of the greathouse roof, a great expanse of slippery tile. Chimneys thrust up from it like stumps. So many of them. Smoke plumed from a few. She looked down a cold one. Remembering Fallo's amusement at her idea to wedge the blade into one, she now understood why. These chimneys were huge. In Cheapsgate, a chimney was nothing more than narrow pipe through the roof. In Terriside, they were wider, made of brick, but still narrow enough the blade would have wedged in nicely. Not these.

She could fit in one. She considered trying it. Maybe she could scurry down and get out while everyone was gathered in Elise's room. But no. Such an act would tempt Pol too greatly. With her luck, a maid would chose that moment to lay a fire. For the moment she was outside in the fresh air, and if she kept quiet, nobody would find her.

At the front of the greathouse, carriages were rolling away, their draft-atlens squawking softly. Though Kila couldn't see them, she heard two people call out farewells as the last couple boarded their carriage. From her perch, Kila could see the course of the Street of the Diadem as it descended toward the Baths of Ori, turn sharply east, and pass through the Trialti Arch. The spires of the Cathedral of Til rose up from Dunne Medow Plaza, backed by the Starside Wall, now lit up along its length with mercus lights on the ramparts.

The carriages swiftly reached their destinations and the Diadem was once again quiet. It was getting colder by the minute, and Kila didn't relish the idea of staying on the roof all night. Autumn brought frequent drizzle to Starside, and she'd had enough of being wet and cold.

Nobody but the hounds remained outside as far as she could tell. She slid down a drain gutter, skirted along the ledge, and dropped to Elise's window. The servant had latched it. Irritating. But she'd expected that. The window wasn't well fitted in its case. Her canvas roll came out of her pocket. She plucked a thin flat probe from its little sleeve, and with her tongue in her teeth, worked the latch open.

Once inside she closed the window and went still. It was darker in here than it was outside, and it took her eyes a moment to adjust. She put the probe away and carefully tucked the canvas roll into a pocket. She felt the uprising energy that presaged her mercus vision. She forced it down, taking careful breaths and silently commanding herself to remain calm.

When she was sure she wasn't about to start seeing glowing metal, she peeped out of Elise's room. No sign of Winter, no sign of servants. The house was still.

She would get food, get a book, and get in bed. Nothing more. Oh, and maybe get Oly.

22

OH, DARLING DAGGER

Oly was not in the kitchen when Kila got there at midnight. She made a thorough search of the cabinets, but she suspected he was snuggled up with Mrs. Nanli. She figured he was safer there than in most of Starside.

She shoved food from the larder into her mouth, barely giving her teeth a chance at it. Bread, two raw chicken eggs, a bit of roast meat left over from the servants' Tilsday dinner, and half a platter of a brown sweetbake that made her tear up with pleasure. It was frosted over the top with a sweet, brown substance that was so delicious she wiped up every blob from the platter. Putting fine manners aside, she decided to just lick it clean. Whatever that dish was, she knew she could eat that and nothing else for the rest of her life. She found an urn of milk and poured a cup full. That sweetbake needed a good swish of milk to wash it down.

Remaining alert came second nature to her, but she

had a feel for the house now. The mercus vision wasn't with her, but she noted the faintest creaks and groans of the house responding to wind and time. Those noises were distinct from the complaints of floor-planks under feet. The house slept, and she might as well have been a ghost, free to move about at will as long as she kept away from people's bedsides.

A ten-day, Fallo had said. Maybe less. But no matter. She was warm, dry, full, and reasonably secure. Her biggest enemy now was boredom. Dreams of her future as a recovery agent would have to distract her for time being. Maybe a shop on Sidle street would be too small. If Fallo and Henley lived with them, they'd need a larger place. A house, maybe. The ones on Curling Street in lower Terriside were larger. Nearer to Finta Sahng but away from the tannery stink. She and Wen would have to buy some finer trousers and shirts, perhaps with a touch of embroidery at the collars. And also warm wool cloaks for cold days. Once they had some jobs under their belt and a bit more coin in their safebox, they'd have to hire a woman to keep house and cook. Kila hoped she knew how to make that brown sweetbake of Mrs. Nanli's.

The boys would each have their own room, each with a featherbed like Elise's. That would be expensive, make no mistake. But once Kila and Wen's reputation got around, they'd have no end of work. They'd be able to name their price. Her mercus vision was getting reliable now. So what lock could bar her? None she'd ever seen.

Nax and the other cats would have cream morning and night. The whole clan of them would feast on chicken and fish and a Winternight roast every Tilsday. Just thinking about Winternight with her little family of thieves warmed her heart. Yes. She could wait here a ten-day to secure all that. Or ten ten-days. All her life she'd scraped by in Cheapsgate, waiting for her chance. Well here it was.

Deciding she'd tempted Pol enough for the night, she did her best to toe her crumbs under the stove. She made a quick stop in the butler's pantry to get the dagger, then crept up to the main floor. Surely there were books lying about. The rich treated them like cast off socks, according to Father. She vowed to herself right then that no matter how rich she and Wen got, they would treasure their books.

She poked into a few dim rooms, noting the abundance of valuable items on tabletops and in cabinets. When the time came to leave, she might have to stuff a few odds and ends into a sack. Her friend Critt Sanglo could move quality silver with ease. The main floor wasn't just corridors and rooms. It was a sort of maze of interconnected sitting rooms and galleries. There was very little light to see by, for the mercus lights had been shaded to blackness. Only a hint of moonlight gleamed through the tall windows.

If ever she needed the mercus vision . . . but no. It wasn't just her neck at risk. Wen was relying on her. She went nearer to a bank of windows, keeping low. Looking back into the room she made out divans and armchairs and low tables. Shiny knick-knacks gleamed on every surface. A lot of very breakable items, each worth a fortune.

There was a bookcase at the back of the room, spines of the tomes behind glass cabinet doors. She padded to it, found the case unlocked. It was too dim to read the spines, much less any of the pages.

She hoped these weren't treatises on agriculture or the fish trade. But even if they were, at least she'd have something to help her while away the time. Choosing a thin volume she doubted would be missed, she returned to Elise's room.

She found a candle in a drawer, along with a box of flashtapers. She doubted anyone but the servants would be up before dawn. And they wouldn't be up in the corridors until it was nearing breakfast time for the guests.

She had hours to spare before dawn, so she propped herself on Elise's bed. The book turned out to be a troublesome one. *Ana and Forli* was a story in verse, about forbidden love and the suicides of both lovers. But it was all a tragic misunderstanding! Kila thought the pair were the stupidest people who ever lived . . . as she quietly wept into Elise's coverlet.

Once recovered from this maudlin display she put on Elise's frilliest gown and brought out PiTorro's dagger. With large and passionate gestures, she acted out the final scene. As Ana, she pretended a pillow was her dear sweet Forli, dead by poison. Whispering the last speech of the story, she held the golden weapon aloft:

[Verse]

"Ah me! I thought him asleep,

Thought me his gentle brow soothed by fortunate dreams.

But his chest rises not! His heart beats not!

And this vial, tumbl'd recently here,

Pitched from his slack fingers, yet spills vile vapors to air."

Kila took a vigorous sniff over the brim of a silver goblet she'd taken from downstairs. Eyes going wide, she cried in soft tones:

"Sableroot and raven's hair? Oh Forli! Why drinkest thou this draught when my Chalice o'erflows for thee?

Spill my love upon your life, not your life over love!

Oh, darling dagger, cut this mortal gown a life-spilling seam,

Join me to my love, in Lumne's wakeless dream!"

With a slow, exaggerated thrust, she stabbed the weapon between her arm and flank and flopped dead upon Elise's featherbed. Eyes glimmering from the tremendous romance of the moment, she lay there, heartbroken.

"Elise!" came a woman's voice from the hall. The door swung open.

Kila swept up the candle and blew it out. A woman bearing a lantern stepped into the room, her feet and legs bare beneath the hem of a sleeping gown.

Kila sprang up, dagger in hand. She froze, eyes locked with the intruder. The woman shrieked and backpedaled from the room. Kila dropped and rolled under the bed.

"Til's love, what is it?" called a man. His legs appeared next to the frightened woman's.

She clung to him, shaking. "I heard someone whispering in here. I—I—I *saw* her!"

"It's the wind and a spell of the midnight mind. Come, have a sip of trezz and sleep."

"But I saw her. I saw Elise. Just there by the bed. She had on that lovely blue gown from Radiant Stilmock's spring ball. You know she told me she wanted to be buried in it? I swear upon the heart of Til himself I saw her just now. I had heard her weeping. And I saw her just there. Hooo! She had a dagger. Pale as ivory, tears on her cheeks."

Kila scowled. She hadn't been weeping. Not out loud anyway.

The man took the candle lantern and stepped into the room. He paused a moment, lifted it high, then backed out. "There's no one here. Let's return to bed."

The woman moaned, and Kila finally recognized her. This was the amorous couple from across the hall. The woman wasn't satisfied with the man's cursory inspection. "The bed there. Doesn't it look a bit disturbed."

"By a footman most likely. The Radiant and his wife have easy routines. They have far too many servants. Likely one or two of them know they can nap the day away here undisturbed."

"I think it was Elise. Murdered spirits return to their homes, they say." The woman scratched an itch on her calf with her toe. "Lady Hiolly won't let a soul enter this room. Do you feel how chill it is?"

The man gave a skeptical grunt.

The woman went on in a rush: "I heard Lilli gossiping about it. She thinks Elise's ghost comes here. And I saw what I saw. In her burial gown. She had a dagger. Oh! Do you suppose that's the blade that killed her?"

Silence. Then, "Yes. That is sensible, dear. It must be Elise's ghost." Finally, the man leaned into the doorway. "Pardon us if we disturbed you, Lady Elise. We'll leave you to your haunting."

The woman elbowed the man's gut. He laughed and said something in a deep throated, provocative tone. Kila didn't catch what it was, but the woman giggled and whispered. "Not in here, you rogue!" Muffling more laughs, they closed the door and retreated to their own room.

Kila let out a long breath. Boredom had always gotten her into trouble. Resolving to be more cautious, she squirmed from under the bed, tidied the covers, and went into the closet.

23

THE TEMPEST

The Hargothe's note came in the middle of the night. Dunne Skyll answered a knock at the door to find a bleary-eyed maid holding the message tube. She yawned hugely. "An acolyte brought it, Dunne Skyll." She made an awkward curtsy. "Apologies for waking you."

Skyll took it, but the girl didn't depart. He raised a questioning eyebrow.

"Would you like tea? Breakfast won't be ready for hours, but there's always muffins for early risers." He nodded and closed the door.

The message tube's cap was sealed with black wax. That alone was dire. The imprint of Til's Hand stood out in sharp relief. The crown over the middle finger made it Highest Chilow's seal.

The paper roll was thin but fine, cut from expensive Jallisea sheet. Skyll was familiar with Highest Chilow's sharp-edged hand, the barely legible scrawl of a man who could scarcely be bothered. This was not Chilow's hand.

It was a scribe's. "Sigh is in Gristenside. Your daughter visits me this morning."

No signature.

None was needed. The first sentence was clear enough. The Hargothe must have felt Sigh upon the mercusine. The second part of the message was about Dorlina, Skyll's secret daughter, sired a ten-year ago upon a widow in Upper Terriside. She had sought his counsel after her husband's death. They'd soon discovered common joys, of dry wines, sourloaf, and the romantic writings of Dol Garilyn. Too much of all three led to a weakening of the formal tone that must apply between parishoner and clergyman. The charms of candlelight and poetry had illuminated her face, and he accepted on reflex a parting kiss on the cheek one evening. She had paused after, the merest hesitation. A moment where her lips and his occupied a range close enough to sense each other's heat.

The maid returned with a tray. He took little notice of her arrival or departure.

He was still in that moment. The kiss had been soft, almost paternal. The widow was young enough to be his daughter. Yet their lips lingered a fraction too long. Had he been slow to retreat? Or had she? And which of them had decided to chance a second, unchaste kiss? Even now he didn't know. What followed that night, and for many a night since, was the indulgence he'd longed for his entire adult life. Not merely in carnal pleasure, but of delight in a simple, domestic life. He'd kept his family hidden from the Way of Til, aided greatly by the freedom of movement allowed a Donse Master of his rank and role. He regretted none of it. Dorlina had been born in due course. A bright-eyed, merry child.

And now the Hargothe knew of her. Surely he had pulled the knowledge from Skyll's brain with his hateful mercusine probes. Dunne Skyll shoved his tray aside. The cups and kettle smashed onto the floor. The serving girl came running. Skyll upended the table. The girl fled.

The proprietor confronted him next. Appell was flustered, red of face, and still in his nightshirt. He stuttered about his other patrons, the expense of good dishes, and the reputation he'd worked a lifetime to establish in the Westreach. Dunne Skyll growled at him and flared his mercus light into existence. The man gibbered and made fearful apologies as he stumbled from the room.

The tempest didn't so much calm as it submerged. Skyll schooled his face, steadied his breathing. With curt orders he got Dunne Postin roused and stuffed into his carriage. "She's in Gristenside," he told the old man and then instructed the driver to take Postin along the Street of the Diadem to sniff out PiTorro's dagger.

Skyll got into his own carriage and followed. The armsmen assembled to escort the carriages. The atlens squawked and sent plumes of frosty breath into the early morning air.

Inside, Dunne Skyll gathered his rage, turning its

power to focus his attention. The Hargothe deserved death for the mere threat. There was no truer thing than that. But Skyll could not accomplish that. Not yet, anyway. The Sigh girl was the cause of all this trouble. He would capture her, of that he had no doubt. If his daughter was harmed, Skyll vowed to slay Sigh in front of the Hargothe's as recompense.

24

OF THE BASEST SORT

He said what? Kila sent.

Nax had come close enough to communicate an hour before dawn. Cats and boys were on the roof of the tea house in Dunne Medow Plaza. Safer than the Street of the Diadem, but still risky, for the rules of the roofway weren't respected around the Plaza.

He said he had no need of a recovery agent, Nax sent. *He says the blade has been recovered.*

I'm holding it in my hand right now.

I know.

Wen might have made a rare mistake with this scheme. He'd approached Tarek PiTorro last night instead of waiting for his Donse Master's search to fail at the Hiolly's front gate. Kila knew why he'd done it. He was worried about her. He was too protective. She loved him, but at the moment she wanted to throttle him. His rush also meant he didn't trust her to not get caught.

Tell Wen he should have been more patient.

He's not close enough for Oly to hear.

Wen's not with you?

He's in an atlen barn. Very weak. Away from Oly too long.

The barn was Fallo and Henley's old place. Before taking up stealing, they had somehow finagled jobs as roost hands, shoveling atlen dung for an egg operation. They lived in the loft. Wen was there because the den wasn't safe.

Wen wants you to leave the blade and bring Oly out, Nax sent.

What do you mean that he's weak?

Henley says he has a . . . fever. Coughing, blood. It was clear from Nax's tone that she didn't know what a fever was. But she knew how grave the blood was. *Fallo says they got something from Finta. He says you have to pay her back.* This last sentence also confused Nax, but not Kila. And it infuriated her. Not the debt itself. Finta wasn't miserly, nor did she ask for much beyond her medicine's cost. Kila was furious at the situation. They had everything in place for their scheme to work. Everything except time.

She would have to find a good hiding spot for the dagger, then get Oly to Wen. Hopefully that would strengthen him long enough that she and the boys could pick some more pockets. Their operation at the Trialti had worked well enough. They could do it at Chance's Corner.

But the house was beginning to wake. Servants

were moving about the hallways in preparation for the Hiolly's and their guests to rise.

I'll come out tonight, she sent.

Good. Wait! There something . . .

She didn't have much choice, so she sat in Elise's closet and fidgeted with the dagger. She'd gotten quite skilled twirling it.

Donse Masters are coming! Nax sent. *Two carriages through the Trialti. Huff says Henley says it's the ones from last night.*

Kila jumped up and considered her options. There weren't any good ones. She suddenly felt stifled and prickly in the closet. She needed air. Needed to see what was going on. She left Elise's room by way of the window and climbed to the roof.

Autumn in Starside was Kila's favorite time of year, but the predawn air this morning held an unseasonable chill. It didn't help Kila's mood that she was hungry again. A pang of jealousy for Oly's coddling took hold. She hoped Mrs. Nanli's excessive feedings gave him a belly ache.

The Donse Masters' carriages rolled to a stop before the front gate. There was no guard on duty at this hour. The draft atlens squawked. The riders' horses stamped wearily, breath pluming from their nostrils. A man climbed down from a horse and rattled the gate.

But then the Hiolly's dogs started barking. Apparently they were left loose on the grounds all night. A disheveled servant emerged from the front entry and hustled to the gate. Words were exchanged and the man ran back to the house. By and by a Hiolly armsman came to have the same conversation, resulting in the same hurried retreat.

Finally, the gate was opened and three men were admitted. Two men in Donse Master's robes and a thickly built man wearing black gloves. His bald head shone in the mercus light.

"Bald as an atlen egg," Kila said to herself. The description matched the man who had chased Fallo after she'd taken the dagger. He was PiTorro's hatchet man, Yilo Chuff. He seemed quite agitated by Dunne Postin's shuffling pace, but he did not rush the man. The other Donse Master, Dunne Skyll, simply outpaced them. Postin appeared to be a hundred years old. He leaned on a cane with one hand and held onto Chuff's arm with the other. He had the unmistakable stride of someone whose vision had mostly failed.

They joined the other Donse Master at the house's front entry. The door opened, they went in, the door closed. They were inside. Kila was not. All she had to do was slide down a downspout, sprint to the wall, and scramble over it.

Except for all those armsmen on their horses just outside the gate. And that Oly was still somewhere inside. So back inside she went too and out into the hallway. This floor was still quiet. Kila slunk down the carpeted hall to the top of the wide stairwell leading down to the front hall. It was a high ceilinged entry foyer, itself big enough to host a formal ball.

Her thieves'-step was second nature; the carpet was thick. She moved as silently as a ghost, senses alert for the slightest footfall, or sneeze, or hound's whimper.

The stairs curved down in three flights to the black and white tiled floor. An enormous crystal chandelier hung over it, shedding sparkles of mercus light like liquid diamonds over the small gathering below.

She stopped on the first landing and froze. Skyll, Postin, and Yilo Chuff were facing off with two men, a man in livery Kila guessed was Mr. Flad the butler. And an elderly lord in a satin knee-length jacket. Radiant Hiolly. Behind him stood yet another Donse Master. He kept well back of Hiolly, hands folded into his sleeves. The clank of Hiolly's armsmen echoed in the hall, but they were blocked from Kila's view by the stairs.

She pulled back from the railing and crouched. If she couldn't see them, they couldn't see her. The only risk now was of someone coming down behind her. Not worth it. The men were speaking in low tones, all rumbles with no consonants. She needed a better eave-dropping spot.

She backtracked to the servant stair. She crept down to the first landing where a door gave into the residence. The men's voices came to her, echoey and distant. There was a short hallway here giving into the parlor from which she'd stolen the book. It was empty. Her bare feet pressed the tile, rolling from toes to heel. Delicate, soft, silent.

Someone had unshaded a mercus light here. The gilded frames and carved-foot furniture gleamed. There were glass figurines on every table, statues in niches, and covering the grand hearth. Opposite the fireplace was a passage that opened directly into the grand foyer. The closer she crept, the clearer the voices became.

"So what you're saying is that one of those in my employ has robbed Mr. PiTorro of his weapon and brought it here. But also that said thief first traipsed down to Cheapsgate, then proceeded to cavort all around Terriside before bringing the blade here." That had to be Radiant Hiolly offering a concise summary of events. His was an old-man's voice, quavery, but tinged with humor.

A hard, deep-throated man responded: "Tarek PiTorro acknowledges the inconvenience. He has instructed me to offer reasonable recompense for imposing on you."

"Has he now?" Hiolly chuckled and conferred with someone in unintelligble mutters. Kila thought it likely to be his house Donse Master. Kila desperately wanted to use her mercus vision, but that was out of the question.

"The blade is that way," Postin declared in a cracked whisper.

"I will have my men investigate. Chuff, you and

Dunne Postin may leave. If we find your master's blade we'll discuss recompense. Captain Sirly escort these gentlemen to their conveyance."

The stomp of a dozen armsmen resounded in unison. Chuff said, "I'll go, Radiant Hiolly. But perhaps you'll allow Dunne Postin to be guided by a man of your choosing, to direct you to the exact location of the blade." The words had a clipped, restrained quality, as if spoken through clenched teeth. Chuff didn't sound like a man used to negotiating compromises.

"Not necessary. The honorable Donse Master has pointed us in the general direction. My household staff are thorough. Captain Sirly, see these gentlemen out."

There were more protests, but Kila caught a glimpse of Chuff moving toward the door. Soon the armsmen and two of the visitors were gone.

Dunne Skyll remained.

"And how may I assist you, Dunne Skyll?" Radiant Hiolly asked. "I must admit, your coming here with Dunne Postin and Yilo Chuff has reduced my opinion of you. They are PiTorro's men and PiTorro is a scoundrel of the basest sort."

Kila mouthed the insult, *"Scoundrel of the basest sort,"* storing it away for later use. It would be fun to say that to Fallo. Not only would he laugh, but he'd admit it was true.

Dunne Skyll said, "I did not accomapny them for PiTorro's benefit. I came as official envoy of the Way of Til."

Hiolly said nothing.

"The one who took PiTorro's blade is still here. I know this because the thief is a merculyn on the verge of awakening to her power. I must take her with me to the cathedral."

"A woman merculyn? No one in my household fits your description. Dunne Ko'ak would have surely noticed."

"Indeed I would have, Radiant. But we must listen to Dunne Skyll. I know him. I doubt he would impose upon you without good reason. He is a Seeker of some note." The man's raspy voice hewed contempt out of the compliment.

"The thief is not in your employ," Skyll said. "She is a Cheapsgater."

"What?" Hiolly said. "Impossible. The Watch wouldn't allow such a creature past the Trialti Arch."

"She is a known thief, with great skill in stealth."

Kila couldn't help but nod in agreement. She *was* skilled in stealth, even if Wen didn't think so.

The Radiant let out a hearty laugh from a deep belly. "A merculyn thief from Cheapsgate is loose in my house? I find this all rather incredible."

"As Dunne Ko'ak so generously noted, I am a Seeker. When our thief holds the mercus, I can feel her quite distinctly, and from a greater distance than usual. I'm surprised, Dunne Ko'ak, you haven't felt her already."

Kila hated Dunne Skyll, but she could appreciate a return barb and Skyll's was deftly delivered.

"My sensitivity to one's mercus potential is not as

great as yours," Ko'ak said. "Hence I am not a Seeker. I don't customarily search for latent talent here without cause, save for my yearly inspection of household staff. In my tenure here I have sent three to the Abbey to become acolytes, have I not, Radiant Hiolly?"

"Relax, Ko'ak. I'm sure Dunne Skyll didn't meant to accuse you of neglecting your duty. Dunne Skyll, where is this vagrant girl now?"

Silence.

Finally, "She does not hold the mercus at the moment. I must draw nearer to her to feel her potential. With your permission, I will quarter the household."

"I will allow it. But if this thief does possess PiTorro's dagger, I want it. That bastard connives to take my Radiancy when I die. I wish nothing for him save ruin. Merchants like him are the worst sorts of climbers there are. I'd give this house to your Cheapsgate thief before I'd give PiTorro a cup of my piss."

There was a bit of uncomfortable laughter. Much of it Kila's, though stifled in the crook of her elbow.

"Ko'ak, accompany Dunne Skyll. See that he has free access to every corridor and closet."

"Yes, Radiant Hiolly."

"Mr. Flad, what do you make all this? How could we have a thief in the house?"

"It is quite impossible, Your Excellency. There has been an error."

"Then what of PiTorro's dagger? If was wasn't

Skyll's thief girl who took it, then one of the staff stole the weapon. They must be turned over to Captain LiTishke's Watch. Can't have thieves aboard, can we?"

"Certainly not, my lord. Dunne Postin pointed to the north parlor. None of my staff would be so daft as to hide their treasure where I would certainly find it."

"Were *you* thieving in Dunne Medow Plaza on Tilsday morn, Mr. Flad?"

Both men laughed.

Soft footsteps on tile warned Kila that someone was approaching. She retreated on silent feet and slipped down the servants' stair. She paused at the opening to the kitchen. This was where she'd first entered the house. A good place to leave it, too, except she didn't have Oly.

The butler was coming down the stairs. She continued along the hallway, away from the kitchen entry. Doors on the left, maybe offices or storerooms.

Nax, where is Oly?

Asleep.

Wake him up!

He refuses. He's warm and full of . . . Nax trailed off, at a loss for words to explain some quality of a sleepy cat's mind.

Kila continued to the end of the hall and rounded the corner just as the butler reached the bottom of the stairs. She pressed her back to the wall and peeked around.

The pantry door was open. The butler was inside. Kila pulled her head back. She wished she'd gone back to Elise's room. She liked being able to escape to the roof. Not knowing where those Donse Masters had gone, she was uncertain where to go next.

The door to the outside was just a quick sprint away. She was sure she could get over the wall before any dogs or armsmen discovered her. She had the dagger with her, if it came to fighting. But without Oly, fleeing was no choice at all. And taking the dagger off Hiolly property would simply draw Dunne Postin and Yilo Chuff after her.

The butler came out of his pantry. She heard the door close. There was silence. He was simply standing there. She didn't dare peek around the corner. The mercus vision wanted to return. The feeling was distinct now, a buzzing in her limbs and head. But catching it before it happened gave her the choice to accept or deny it. Ah, but it was hard to deny. She needed it. If she accepted it, she could simply watch the butler's vest buttons and shoe buckles to see where he went.

But she didn't dare to with Dunne Skyll in the house.

Footsteps told her of the butler's retreat up the servants' stair. Kila sagged against the wall for a moment. Her stomach relaxed, then growled so loudly she tried to muffle it with her hand.

After pilfering some bread and cheese from the larder, she crept to the servants' stair and made it safely to Elise's room. She wanted nothing more than to hide among the gowns in the closet and enjoy her breakfast, but she would be cornered there if Skyll came in.

She locked Elise's door and huddled beneath the unlatched window. She ate her bread and cheese in huge mouthfuls. No enjoying it, just getting it down. She imagined the Donse Masters creeping through the hallway, using their weird magic to feel her out.

Skyll kept saying she was awakening to the mercus. She didn't truly know what that meant. Aside from the mercus vision, she'd no experience with the mercusine. She'd never performed a feat of power. And she didn't want to. Such would land a girl in the Baths of Ori, dressed like a trollop and made to perform all manner of lustful rituals beneath the moonlight. Or so she'd heard.

She recalled what that hateful skeletal man had said into her thoughts: *You will serve Til through me.*

That sounded worse than a life at the Baths. He meant to keep her in the Way of Til. But there were no female acolytes or Donse Masters and never would be. Skyll himself had claimed to pity Kila for what was in store for her at the hands of the mind-speaking invalid.

The doorknob rattled.

Kila jerked upright. The rasp of key in lock drove her out the window. She nudged it closed with her foot as she climbed up the rain gutter. Once again she peered down as the window swung open. This time it was Skyll who stuck his head out. The wind tousled his gray locks as he remained there, very still. Then he craned his neck to look up.

Kila crabwalked out of his view before he saw her. She hadn't been holding the mercus vision, but maybe that didn't matter when he was that close. Shivering from more than the icy wind, she traversed the greathouse's roof pitches, putting as much distance as she could between her and Skyll.

25

A LITTLE NEST

Dunne Skyll pulled his head back through the window. For a moment he'd felt something out there. Too faint and fleeting to be sure. The bedroom smelled faintly of cheese and bread. Odd for a supposedly vacant room. "Dunne Ko'ak, do servants idle away the hours in here to avoid chores?"

"None who do remain employed." Dunne Ko'ak was pudgy, soft. Assignment as a House Donse Master was considered a career achievement, a chance for an ambitious Donse Master to earn the favor of a wealthy and influential sponsor. But most found the comforts of the post so enticing that their loyalties shifted from the Way and toward comfort, wine, and food. "Are you certain the thief is still here?"

"I thought I felt something in this room." Skyll turned back to the window, peered out over the rear park, a well kept lawn surrounded by woodlands and a few structures. The Hiolly armsmen were returning to their barracks having escorted Dunne Postin and

Yilo Chuff off the premises. Skyll hadn't allowed himself to enjoy Postin's ill treatment. Radiant Hiolly's dismissive mein showed just how powerful such men were. Skyll touched the window latch. "This window wasn't secured when I came in," he said. "I thought I sensed someone on the roof just above."

"So our mercyulyn can fly, can she?" Ko'ak said. "Perhaps you need a rest, Dunne Skyll. I can have a room prepared for you."

"Send a man onto the roof."

Ko'ak didn't move to comply. There was a rigidity in him, like that of a stubborn horse who hated the bit. Skyll had no time for a challenge of seniority. In the Way of Til, one's years in service granted a sort of unofficial authority. But power overruled all. Power in the mercus, and power in the hierarchy of the clergy.

"I am the agent of the Hargothe, Dunne Ko'ak," he said. "The great seer will learn of your involvment in this endeavor, for good or ill."

The man's stiffness increased, but he relented. "I will send a man onto the roof." He went out of the room. A low conversation occurred and a servant went running.

Dunne Skyll scanned the shrouded furniture. The bedclothes were not as tidy as one would expect in a house of this quality. He focused his mind and brought forth a sphere of mercus light over his head. He sent it down to illuminate the floor beneath his feet. Crumbs. He squatted and dabbed up a few. Bread.

He went to the closet and sent his light in. Gowns

wadded on the floor. An empty bottle. A platter with an apple core and more crumbs. Sigh had made herself a little nest. He considered her decision to come here, of all places in Starside. It seemed she had known that PiTorro was disliked in this house and that his men would be dismissed. And somehow Sigh knew the blade was being tracked.

The ridiculous chase up and down the Sorrows made more sense now. She had done it to exhaust Dunne Postin. Ko'ak returned. "A man is being roused to fetch a ladder. Do you truly think she's on the roof?"

"You will remain here in case she tries to escape back indoors."

"Are you going onto the roof?"

Dunne Skyll considered it. He didn't love heights. But he feared the Hargothe more. But going onto the roof would not be necessary. "No. I will continue my search indoors." He walked out, relishing Ko'ak's frustration. Skyll well knew the insult the old man would feel at being ordered to remain behind. And that was good, for Skyll was starting to see a post for himself here in this greathouse as a possible retirement. Perhaps the Hargothe would reward him when he brought the girl back. Assuming Skyll didn't have to kill her out of vengeance for Dorlina.

A servant was waiting just outside the room. Skyll said, "Take me to the attics."

26

OF HOUNDS AND RAVENS

The men were carrying a ladder over their shoulders. Kila watched them from her hiding spot behind a chimney. A needling rain blew horizontally on a stiff wind that carried hints of winter. The men would be up here very soon. She retreated to the front side of the house. There were gutters and downspouts here. She could get down quickly and hide in the gardens, or perhaps make a dash around the house and try to cross the lawn to the trees.

Except the hounds were still out. They went in patrols with armsmen carrying storm lanterns. They were quartering the estate in search of tresspassers. A sensible move considering Yilo Chuff's visit. Mustn't have thieves lingering about, after all. It was quite dark in the front gardens despite the moonlight, for the open areas were hemmed in with copses of trees casting deep shadows. An enormous wireoak spread its canopy over a third of the grounds fronting the

Street of the Diadem. She counted lanterns. Three pairs. Each patrol had two men and two hounds on leashes.

The front of the house was relatively well lit with mercus lights. She'd be seen if she tried to climb down here. The men would release their dogs and she'd never outrun them. And even if she managed to hide or escaped into that tree, their noses would lead the men right to her.

She slunk back over the ridge of the roof and climbed down to Elise's window. The ledge here was negligible and her toes were growing numb from the cold. She managed to peer into Elise's room. It was dark. The window was still slightly ajar. She opened it and swung herself in.

The second her feet touched the thick carpet beneath the window, her hair lifted from her neck. Skyll had leaned out to look around. He wouldn't have left it unlocked.

Light bloomed near the ceiling, a dot of bluish-white. The covered furniture cast sharp shadows onto the floor. Kila blinked hard.

"Barefoot and holding a stolen blade." The Donse Master came toward her, hands tucked into opposite sleeves. His face was doughy and sparsely whiskered. Too young and stout to be Dunne Postin. This had to be Dunne Ko'ak, the House Donse Master. Kila looked for Skyll and his hateful little wand. But Ko'ak was alone. He wrinkled his nose. "Ah, but your mercus is indeed loud. Come here, child. I won't hurt you."

How many times had Kila heard those same words

in Cheapsgate? It was the first thing alley-gropers said. He was even smiling in the oily way of weak and lustful men. Once again a man was underestimating his own danger because he thought her a mere scrawny girl. And yet she had a dagger in her hand.

That puzzled her, and she cautiously circled away from him. She didn't raise the weapon. If she could get the right angle to the door she would just slip away.

A man stepped into the doorway, a sillhouette against the mercus light in the hallway. "Dunne Ko'ak, the men are on the roof. They haven't found—"

"Call them down. Fetch Dunne Skyll at once."

But the man spotted Kila. He barked something over his shoulder and remained where he was. He wasn't an armsman and had no weapon, but he was big enough to bar an easy escape.

Kila's hand tightened on the hilt of PiTorro's blade. It truly was a fine weapon. And it didn't feel ceremonial now. She hoped Fallo hadn't been exaggerating about its deadly qualities. Because its supposed demaynic powers were about to be tested.

"I don't want to cut you," she said. Her voice sounded odd to her own ears, distant but firm. Deep and commanding.

"Attack and you forfeit your life," Ko'ak said. "Think, girl. You are on the verge of awakening to the mercus. A wonderful life of advantage awaits you. You might one day be a Voluptuary or even a Coin of Pol. Yes, I feel it surging in you now."

Strong words, but he took a half step back at the end. Kila had faced bullies and angry marks many times. That little retreat told her all she needed to know. Ko'ak had no ability to fight her, even with his mercus.

She moved toward him. His light flared. She raised her arm to shield her face against the blaze. Footsteps warned of someone rushing toward her. She crouched and lashed out with the blade.

It struck, a jolt carried down her arm. A heavy weight crushed onto her. It was the man from the doorway. He gripped her wrist, twisted hard to wrest the dagger from her hand. She kicked, caught a sensitive spot. His fight ceased. She yanked her wrist free and jabbed, once, twice. Grunts of pain fluttered from his lips.

Stumbling blindly, she charged the Donse Master. The light was too bright. Eyes closed, she saw a gold necklace, a purse with a few coins, a pin on his robes.

Thundering footsteps sounded directly above her. Someone upstairs was running. More calls were rising in the rooms around her. A woman kept asking what was going on in ever shriller tones.

The house was awakening. Kila charged toward the Donse Master. She lunged with her dagger. Ko'ak stumbled aside and she let momentum carry her onward and through the door. Metal sconces on the walls, brass doorknobs, candlesticks. She raced to the servants' stair, barged through the door.

Down, down to the kitchen hall. Pots and pans and silver and more doorknobs. Iron stove, spit rods, kettles, cauldrons, and tin buckets. Shoe buckles and belt buckles and buttons. People yelled, some shrieked.

"Hey there!"

"Stop!"

"What is the meaning of this?"

"Thief!"

"Murder!"

"Murder!"

Kila shoved through the kitchen door and into the garden beyond. Off to her left was a man descending a ladder. The kitchen garden was enclosed by a low wall. Kila made for the little shed. Stopped short of it, remembering the hounds. They'd find her there and she'd be trapped.

The dagger was still her her hands. She paused, battling two thoughts. A lifetime of thieving was sending jangles of warning through her mind. To be caught with a weapon was tenfold worse than to be caught without one. But to be rid of it would leave her defenseless.

She'd already used it. She'd cut someone. With or without it her life was over if captured. If not the Way of Til, the Watch would take her.

The ladder man hadn't seen her. But a footman was coming out of the kitchen behind her wielding a huge iron skillet. She leapt the garden wall and skirted along it, away from the house. The armsmen's barracks stood off to her left. Across a gravel paved carriage lot was the atlen barn, beyond it another structure loomed in the slanting rain. Kila darted behind the barn. Shouts grew fainter behind her. The footman lost his commitment to battle and did not give chase.

Dogs bayed in the distance. They would catch her scent. They would follow her.

She raced along the rear of the barn, paused at the corner. No one in view. The land sloped up to a knoll where the next building stood. She darted across the gap to the shadows behind it. This was a stonework building in a different style to the others. She couldn't see anything here, for she'd come among dense trees. There was little haze of metal through the building's walls. Dragging one hand along the stonework, she felt her way forward. All her senses were alert to the sound of dogs and men. The mercus vision had come over her without warning back in Elise's room. She knew that Dunne Skyll could use that to track her as surely as her scent drew the dogs. But she needed it.

Rain hissed into the leaves still on the trees. Her feet ached from the cold and the wind found its way down her collar. She had to find a place to hide. A place to get warm.

Her fingers drifted across the stone. So smooth. The mortar here was different than on the house, smoother, tighter. She recognized it then as the work of the First Race, of elnisians. This structure was older than the greathouse itself. Something about it pulled at her attention. It was too dark to see any detail here. There were no windows or doors on the back of the building.

The dogs were louder now. The men had gone silent. They were letting the hounds do their job. Kila jabbed the dagger into the dirt and wiped her palm on her trousers. If she had to fight, she didn't want to lose her grip. She took the weapon back up and went forward and rounded the building. There she stopped.

A break in the clouds exposed the moon, though rain still clung to all of Gristenside. She paused there at the edge of moonshadow, drawing the tiniest sense of protection from the trees. The dogs were getting much closer now. She didn't want to hurt any dogs. She loved dogs. But she would fight them if she had to. Anyone would. Something glinted on the wall above her. She craned her neck to see a steel pipe extending from the building.

It was too high to reach by jumping, and the wall was not scalable. Kila backed away from the building and into the trees. The dogs were coming.

She spotted it then. A branch overhanging the roof.

The tree was a thick elm or ash. Kila was a city girl, and to her one tree was pretty much the same as another. The autumn change had not yet stripped it of its leaves. The bark was rough and shaggy. It made for easy climbing.

Three dogs found her halfway to the limb. They surely couldn't see her, but they smelled her. Thinking they had her treed, they went into a frenzy of yelping and barking and pawing at the tree trunk. The men would come in force now.

She reached the limb and paused a moment to breathe and assess the likelihood of dying. The drop was ten spans. If she fell, it wasn't certain she be instantly killed. The dogs might have their chance to rip out her throat while she lay in the leaves with two broken legs. The limb was thick, but dead.

The roof was flat.

One, two, three, four steps. A crack in the limb. She jumped, landed on the roof and rolled. The dogs didn't notice her stunt. But it wasn't an escape if she couldn't get down. She dropped to all fours and scrambled to the far edge. Laying flat she peered into the vast grassy lawn. Armsmen were approaching in loose groups. They were walking fast with their storm lanterns held up. Far beyond were the sparks of two floating spheres of mercus light, one larger than the other. The Donse Masters.

The break in the clouds sealed shut, muting the moonlight. The wind snarled and needled Kila with ice flecks. Her rag shirt and trousers offered no protection now that they were soaked through with rain and sweat.

"Kil's eyes in a bucket!" she rasped, shivering. Withdrawing from the edge, she turned her attention to the roof and its surroundings. The only way down was to drop from the roof to that jutting pipe. Then from it to the ground. She peeped down at it. No good. Two men were standing there, swords and lanterns in hand. More men were gathering around the dogs.

If she could get the men below her to leave she might have a chance to descend and dash across the lawn to the deeper woods beyond. Eventually she'd come to the wall separating the Hiolly estate from their neighbors. She could climb over.

But to distract the men required having something to hurl into the trees. The only thing she had was the dagger.

"I don't see her!" said a man. He sounded very nearby. "Wait! I think I see a limb over the cistern."

They had sent a man up the tree. Kila cast about for a bit of debris, perhaps a blown limb or stick she might throw down to distract the men in her way. It seemed such a weak idea, the last hope.

A glow of steel drew her eye. It was very faint. Ah, a continuation of the pipe inside the building. And that wasn't the only metal here. There was a grate embedded in the roof. Her fingers swept over the surface beneath her. For the first time the material of the roof registered. It was tile. And it wasn't flat. It was graded to carry rainwater inward, away from the edge of the roof.

Cistern! This whole building was a water giant catch. She scurried to the grate and lifted. It squealed in complaint.

"What was that?" called a man from below.

The metal was slick and cold. She found the top rung of a ladder, and that was all she needed. "Just like the sewers," she said to herself as she went down, easing the grate closed over her. She tucked the dagger into the waist of her trousers. The weight of it threatened to pull her pants down.

There was nothing to see below; the darkness here was absolute. Her mercus vision showed her the pipe very clearly now. Its opening was as wide as her head, and it apparently hung over empty space above the floor. Odd.

She continued down. The rungs were not metal, but carved into the stone wall. She reached with her toes and went down and down. The air was cold, like a root cellar. She lost count of the rungs, but the glowing pipe was a good reference. Soon it was high above her. And then her feet encountered water. Frigid. She plunged down two more rungs. Three. Still no floor. Four. Five. Still no bottom. The building was full of water. It was now over her waist, icy, relentless. Voices above her. The grate was a square of gray in the blackness.

And then that went away. Someone was standing over it, blocking the moonlight. She released the ladder and shoved off. The cold embraced her, made her gasp and shiver. She stroked into the darkness, then treaded water.

It was too cold. She couldn't stay here.

The grate swung open and clanged like a dissonant bell. "It's black as Kil's own heart in here!"

The voice resounded, echoey and hollow in the cistern. Kila floated on her back and went still.

"Hand me up a lantern and a rope." Then, "She had to have. Where else could she have gone?"

The dogs had continued their barking despite the men admonishing them to be still. For some reason they suddenly lost their minds and doubled their barking frenzy. The noise faded even as their baying grew more irate.

Men shouted for Bruiser and Crusher and Mauler

to come, to heel, to stay, to sit. By the sound of their fading racket, they had gone deaf to all commands.

"What's got into them?" called the man on the roof. "What? But how did she get down from the trees?" Kila's jaw started to quiver, her sides shook, her belly cramped from the cold. "Oh. Then I'm coming down." The grate slammed to and the patch of sky reappeared.

Surely Dunne Skyll had gotten to the building by now. But now she realized her mercus vision had vanished. The grate didn't glow and neither did the pipe. And with the dogs tailing off on some false scent, the Donse Masters had surely followed.

False scent. She couldn't concentrate. She had to get out of the cistern, and even then she'd be too cold. No thinking. If she thought too long, she'd die in here. She had to move and keep moving.

She found the stone rungs and managed to pull herself up. She had to go by pressure on her hands and feet alone, for they were numb to everything else. Dripping and shivering, she climbed. At the top, she didn't bother to pause and listen. She was going to die if she stayed where she was.

Pushing with her head, she lifted the grate and squirmed through. She set it softly closed and took in the situation. Nobody on the roof. She went back to the tree limb. It was cocked at a sharp angle. She couldn't trust it to support her weight.

Back to the pipe jutting from the wall. She understood it's purpose now. An overflow outlet in case the cistern filled. She imagined such was possible in spring. It had been good fortune for her that it was so empty now.

There were no men about. She wouldn't risk the mercus vision to look for weapons and armor among the trees. From this point on, she would do nothing to draw Skyll's attention. She was about to lower herself over the pipe when the weight of the dagger pulled her trousers half off her hip.

She hadn't done all this to simply lose it or take it off the estate and draw Dunne Postin to it. Scrambling back to the grate, she dropped the dagger into the cistern. A musical splash answered her. When PiTorro decided to pay, she would be able to recover it easily enough. Wouldn't even have to go into the greathouse.

The pipe was wider than many ledges she'd jumped to on her roofway runs, but usually she could feel her feet. No time. She lowered herself, and let go. She landed softly, with only a low resonance in the pipe to report the impact. She went on hands and knees to the end of the pipe. She swung out, dangled from it until she steadied, then dropped to the ground.

No stopping to check if she'd been spotted. She sprang up and ran. She noticed a few flakes of snow on the grass as she sprinted toward the deeper wood beyond the lawn. The trees embraced her with darkness; leaves rustled softly under her steps. She slowed, panting and shivering at the same time. Her soaked clothes burned her skin. She tugged off her shirt and wrung it out as best she could. Shrugging back into it was a torture of ice on her flanks and belly. She squeezed her pant legs as best she could. Her hands weren't working well. Getting rid of the dagger was the smartest thing she'd done so far.

Being cold was not new. Living in Cheapsate had conditioned her to it. But this . . . This chill was a knife edge poised above her very existence. Move, Sigh, she told herself. Move!

She moved, picking her way on feet that could not feel the ground under them. She flailed for support against tree trunks now. Her teeth chattered, what housemothers called the "Chillbone Song." They claimed that bones bargained with the cold in a language no mortal could understand.

The wall struck her toe first, and in that way spared her nose. She leaned against it, rubbing her arms and trying to keep moving by bouncing her knees. But her strength was following her body heat into the night air.

Don't give up!

Nax?

Move! Move! Find a warm hole to hide in!

A warm hole? But of course a cat would think that. The sending was very faint, but also intense, like a shout heard at a great distance. Something else came with it. An imperative to move her feet. And so Kila walked along the wall, slowly now. She tucked her hands under her arms, hugging herself.

The wall was high, but stoney, with lots of crevices and toe holds. If she hadn't been so cold, she would have already gone over it. It might as well have been the Divide itself. She was not climbing over it. No chance.

The dogs were screaming very far away. It sounded like they were in the front gardens. Dogs from neighboring kennels had taken up the cause, and Gristenside's peace was ruined by choruses of barking.

Kila stumbled on, moving only because stopping was an assured death. A sort of death she did not want. She wanted to die warm. The ground struck her cheek. Damp leaves stuck to her chin. She wanted to curl up and sleep.

No! Move! Nax sent. How the cat knew she'd fallen was a mystery Kila didn't have the strength to ponder. But she got onto her hands and knees, and then once again onto her feet. The wall turned a sharp angle, forcing her back toward the house. This course would take her through the woods behind the barracks.

The idea of the barracks filled her mind. She recalled the men sitting to dinner, the warm whale-oil lanterns inside. She went faster, pulled now by the idea of warmth. She would crawl into a dragon's mouth right now if it offered her escape from the chill.

The lights of the barracks broke through the trees. She stumbled toward it, not caring about armsmen or dogs or Donse Masters. She fell over a root, got back up, and fell again. She crawled through thorny tangles of dead raspberry canes that plucked at her shirt and trousers. She did not feel the scratches at all. When she was finally free of them, she staggered to the barracks. A woodpile was neatly stacked against the rear wall beneath an overhang. A door next to it. The smell of sweet smoke.

Kila went in. The warmth of the kitchen doubled the chill in her bones. She collapsed and hugged herself and rocked, failing to keep gasps in, failing to keep tears in. The heat came from an iron stove inset into the stone wall. The air smelled of baking bread and stew. Kila forced herself to crawl to the stove, where embers still glowed.

Nobody had heard her come in. But fear of discovery returned, hard. Her feet screamed as she stood. In her numb flight, she had gathered cuts and thorns on the soles of her feet. Now that the numbness was tingling away, the sharp stabs finally registered. She hissed and pinched thorns from her flesh with filthy fingers.

She staggered from the kitchen and into the main hall. There wasn't a soul in the barracks. All were out looking for her. A smile made it to her lips as she crept through the aisles of bunks. An open wooden stair climbed to a second floor. She went up. She didn't know the ranks among companies of private arms-men, but they clearly had a few officers. The largest bedroom was plain, but well appointed. A comfortable bed took up most of it. Chests, an armor stand, and basin took up the rest. Kila wanted nothing more than to climb into the bed and sink into warmth.

The other two bedrooms were smaller, with fewer amenities. One had an attic hatch in the ceiling acces-sible by a crude wooden ladder attached to the wall. Kila stole a spare blanket from the captain's closet and went up. It was dark, musty and cold. But at least there was no wind. The main hall's chimney ran right through it. The bricks shed some warmth. Kila rid herself of her clothes, and hung them over a few sticks of old furniture to dry. She curled into the blanket, shivering, and pressed close to the warm bricks.

The dogs continued to bark in the distance.

I'm safe, she sent to Nax, whose presence had grown much closer since she'd come into the barracks.

Oly is too. It was close.

What do you mean? Oly is snug in the house.

No. He's outside in a tree. The dogs almost got him.

The dogs. Their sudden distraction now made sense. Oly had come out, had lured them away.

Is Wen with you?

No. He is not well. I'm with Fallo and Henley. We are hiding.

Dunne Postin was turned away, just as we hoped. PiTorro will never get his dagger back without our help. I've hidden it well.

Nax pulsed impatience through the bond. *Stay hidden.*

I am! Kil's eyes, the cat was almost as bad as Wen. Did they all think she was stupid? Apparently they did. But none of them were here, facing the threats she was facing. Her shivering subsided again and she felt herself grow sleepy. That was bad.

She retreived her clothes and wrung them out as best she could. Shrugging into them made her gasp and hiss several curses. But it was to tempt Pol to remain naked, even hidden in this attic. She returned to her blanket and pressed close to the chimney.

Is Oly where he can see what the men and dogs are doing?

He is in a tree. They are all around him.

They thought she was in that tree. They would send a man up to search it. Oly was agile and would be difficult to catch, but not as difficult to shoot with a flickbow. So she had a choice. Remain here and rest and wait for her clothes to dry. Or venture out. But to do what? To rescue Oly would require her to lead the dogs and men away.

Stuck in this dilemma she lost track of her choices and slipped into Lumne's realm, and into restless dreams of hounds and ravens.

27

A LESSON TO US ALL

"You are an utter failure, Dunne Ko'ak. Your tenure in the Hiolly greathouse is at risk. If you are fortunate, the Hargothe will allow you to serve out the remainder of your life in the Soral monestary counting pepper seeds and recording the hourly weather."

Dunne Skyll turned his back on the man. Sigh had been in Elise's room and he'd done nothing. Worse, he'd allowed one of Radiant Hiolly's servants to be stabbed.

Radiant Hiolly's wife kept insisting they take the man to the Baths of Ori, but Skyll had forbidden it. Might as well drown the man outright than give him over into the immoral rituals of that band of witches. And now Sigh was gone. Again. These men and these hounds were useless. Surely the girl hadn't climbed up this tree. She was too savvy to allow herself to be cornered.

The tree they had surrounded was an ancient

wireoak, with gnarled limbs themselves as thick as a treetrunks. It had been here since the elnisians had left the city, predating the greathouse by five hundred years. The girl *could* be up there, he supposed. But Skyll didn't feel her mercus potential. The last place he'd felt her was near the old elnisian cistern. One man had thought she'd gone into it. But if so, she was dead by now. He waved an armsman over and told him to go into the cistern just to be sure.

He now had to consider the possibility of facing the Hargothe with news of Sigh's death. Which would leave him no bargaining power for his own daughter's life. If Sigh was dead, Dorlina would be too. Skyll would have to leave Starside this very night. He still had the carriage, atlens, and driver from the Abbey's stable. He would go back to Appel's Inn, sleep through the day, then strike out through the Moriterran Pass at dusk. The Hargothe was powerful in Starside, the master even of Highest Chilow. But his reach did not extend far beyond these walls.

Skyll could go south to Jallisea. There he could buy passage to Garden Island. The Highest of Highests resided there. A man Skyll had known when they were young, Mancin Fley. He would hear of the Hargothe's depredations. There was no man more jealous of power than Highest Fley.

Yes. And since Highest Chilow allowed the Hargothe to pursue his vile projects in Starside, he too would be removed in due course. That would make the vestments of Highest in Starside available to someone new. Surely once those two were killed, the

Thebkine Table would choose Skyll, especially if the mandate came down from Highest Fley.

Skyll's enthusiasm for this scheme dissipated like smoke. He should have thought of all this a ten-day ago. He could not abandon Dorlina or her mother now that the Hargothe knew they existed.

By the time the armsman returned with news that Sigh's body was not in the cistern, Skyll had become so wistful about the impossibility of fleeing Starside, that he was relieved to learn of Sigh's escape.

"I found this," the armsman said, holding up a golden dagger. Skyll took it, turned it this way and that. The gold gleamed as if freshly polished. The blade showed neither nick nor scratch.

"Excellent." He slid the weapon into his satchel. And at the same time shoved the last gleams of his fantasy in with it. Shadowy ambitions crowded into the vacancy, of the Hargothe writhing in agony as Sigh screamed before him, throat cut with PiTorro's blade. That would be justice on both of them.

He stood there in silence for a long time, gazing up at the tree and considering his options. But it was Dunne Ko'ak's gruff clearing of throat that returned him to the present. "I thought I had dismissed you," Skyll said to the man.

"On whose authority?" Ko'ak said. "Surely Seer Hargothe does not care about assignments to Radiancies or monasteries. And though you may slander my name to him or others, none will believe you. I'm your senior by a ten-year, a Donse Master of excellent reputation, with good connections across Gristenside. Had you given as much time to relationships as you have to hunting merculyns, you might also enjoy such influence. Truth be, Dunne Skyll, you are of little consequence, hardly more than a fancy acolyte. You pretend to speak for the Hargothe, but he's granted you no such authority. Your power in the mercus is greater than mine, I'll grant you that, but so what? You can manifest a brighter light than I can. Perhaps you could light a candle were you given a quiet room and an hour to work on it. But that's nothing to boast about." He approached, hands in sleeves, shaking his head in mock sadness. "Truth be, Dunne Skyll, your only real value is in your greater sensitivy to other merculyns. Face it. You aren't even very good at that. So it is I who dissmisses you. You have disrupted the quietude of this Tilsnight for too long. Please leave, else I will instruct these armsmen to carry you out."

Dunne Ko'ak turned his back on Skyll. It was this, more than his pointless harangue, that incensed Skyll and drove him to draw his mercus artifact. The pale rod did not require much effort. Simply an intention, a thread of unfocused mercus, and a target. Dunne Ko'ak tumbled forward as stiff as a statue. Without the freedom of his arms, he could do nothing to protect his face from the fall. It struck the turf beneath the wireoak with a louder crack than Skyll expected.

Skyll went to him, toed him over. Blood pulsed from the man's smashed nose. Skyll grimaced. Ko'ak's face had struck an exposed root. He was not breathing. Skyll knelt and shook him. The man was dead and Skyll felt nothing but satisfaction. "A terrible accident." He pointed to the root. "He tripped. Pol frowns upon the vain and ambitious. Let this be a lesson to us all."

The armsmen looked at each other in alarm. Captain Sirly of the house guard came forward, helm off. He scratched his ear and grimaced. "I suppose I ought to fetch the Radiant."

"Let him be. There is nothing he can do for Dunne Ko'ak. But he will not be best pleased to learn that a thief still trespasses upon his estate. You would do well to find her and bring her to me. Surely these hounds can be herded away from this tree. I assure you our quarry is not in it. These dogs have treed a squirrel. I had expected better training. Radiant Hiolly was once known as a gifted breeder. It would be a pity if I had to tell him of this embarrassing display."

The armsmen's shoulders lifted and their faces went stony at these insinuations. But Skyll's words had the intended effect. The men leashed their dogs and dragged them off. The captain rallied his men and told them off in squads of threes. No inch of the property would escape their scrutinity, he assured Dunne Skyll. The one who found the girl would be rewarded with a paid ten-day leave and a bonus of five gold skillets.

"And I will match that with five skillets from my own pocket," Dunne Skyll said. Ten gold would earn any of these men a ten-day of debauchery unmatched in their lives. And that prospect showed in the new energy that propelled their steps.

Skyll again looked up the tree, puzzled by the

dogs' certainty that Sigh was in it. He sent his sphere of mercus light into the upper boughs. It disturbed an owl, who looked back with squinted disdain before gliding away.

He again considered leaving Starside. But these thoughts were of what he would do after Sigh and the Hargothe were dead. He would take Dorlina with him. Ko'ak's words had wormed into his mind, digging out thoughts he had long kept tamped down. Thoughts of his own insignificance.

As he floated his mercus light down, the glare caught a pair of green eyes. An animal. Too large to be a squirrel, the wrong shape for a possum. Something gleamed from a ribbon around its neck. He sent the sphere toward it, but the animal scrambled around the limb. The tinkling of a little bell went with it. Dead leaves tumbled in a flurry in the wake of its flight. The little bell went silent. But Skyll had seen enough. A hint of whitish fur. A predatory fang. It was a cat, but not the same cat that had attacked him on the Sorrows.

Skyll had never been a particularly religious man. His belief in Til was habitual, but not deep. What he believed in was the inherent depravity of man. Prayer, it had always seemed to Skyll, must surely be too self-interested to be of interest to the gods. So he had not bothered with it for twenty years, outside of formal rites within the Way. But now he uttered a prayer; a heart-felt one. For the presence of two cats in association with Kila Sigh could be no coincidence. That it was adorned with collar and bell confused him a bit. No thief would bring such a noise maker along with them. Still . . . He could not doubt that it was Sigh's ally. What its presence here portended was as ominous and as vague as Moonside itself.

But it explained the dogs' frenzied certainty that Sigh was in the tree. Dogs were notoriously stupid, as evidenced by their drooling loyalty to men. The cat had led them on a merry chase, away from Sigh.

He left the tree and once again circled the greathouse in search of Captain Sirly. He waved him down. "Fetch the groundskeeper. Tell him to bring a ladder and saw to the wireoak in front. Have some footmen come out too, with sheets, or sacks, or nets. And a box. There is an animal in that tree I must have."

He turned his gaze back to the wireoak's upper boughs, which were visible over the roof of the greathouse. The more things he possessed that the Hargothe desired, the more suffering he could inflict upon the old seer in the end.

28

IN A STILLED MOMENT

The ladder creaked, a high pitched squeal that Kila didn't understand at first. She had fallen asleep, but the sound had yanked her up by her collar. The next sound was the groan of the attic hatch. She didn't know how long she'd slept, but her muddled mind and body were not at all refreshed. Her clothes were still damp. The floorboards groaned under a heavy weight. Next came a susurrus of fabric rubbing. Behind that was the presence of a man standing in silence, listening. Kila felt him, envisioned him from the weight of his being. A heavy man with corded arms and barrel chest. He was in the attic with her. He was trying to be very still. Trying to listen. Listening for her presence.

The Donse Master? No. He would not feel so heavy.

The mercus vision was upon her. It had brought with it this heightening of her senses. In the absolute stillness of the darkness, her hearing and smell, and even the feel of the floor beneath her were carrying subtle hints of the man. It was the instinctive awareness of danger that every mouse or deer or lone woman in an alley knew in the gut. It was the feeling of prey in the presence of death.

The floor creaked. She imagined him shifting his weight from one foot to the other. A whisper. Someone in the room below asking what the man saw. He didn't respond.

Through the fabric of her blanket came a blooming light. Someone had handed up a lantern. A footstep, a creak. The rustle of fabric, the jangle of metal buckles, the scuff of a boot on dusty wood.

"Anything?" The whisper was loud, raspy.

Her breath shook on the exhale.

Another step. The light wavered as the man held up his lantern. Even through the knit wool, she saw the rafter shadows stretch and move.

A boot settled next to her head. The toe planted, twisted a bit as he took another step. She heard the dust grind under the sole. His breath whistled softly in his nose.

He was tenative. He'd been told to search the attic. The Donse Master was desperate to find her. Someone had been stabbed. They were told to look everywhere. Had she left a trail? She had been very wet. Surely those drips had dried by now. She'd closed the door behind her. She hadn't left attic hatch open. No one would notice the blanket she'd taken, not when they were all up and searching for her.

No. This was simply a search. He was being thorough. The dogs had trailed off after Oly. The Donse Master had lost her when she'd let go of her mercus vision in the cistern. She needed to remain still.

But he would notice her blanket. What would he see?

It was a clean, tan wool blanket. Summer wool. She was curled up under it. But it was wrapped tightly around her and under her. It would look like a person was in it, not simply a wadded bunch of fabric. He would see her. He had stepped right next to her.

He took two more steps, paused.

Her clothes. He was looking at where she'd hung her clothes. Would there be a puddle there still? Or maybe spots where dust had been wiped clean by her feet. She should never have taken them off. She shouldn't have stayed in the barracks.

"Bring her down!" came a familiar voice. "She's up there right now."

Skyll!

A weight crushed her; arms like iron bands scooped under her. She came off the floor, netted in her own blanket. She screamed and struggled, but she was held fast in a curled up ball. "I have her!" the man shouted. His voice was deep and loud.

He clomped with heavy steps, stopped. "If I let her go she's going to fight."

"Hold a moment."

Panic seized her. She squirmed and screamed, but her captor's arms might as well have been shackles. And then her struggles ceased as an indomitable power took hold of her limbs and stilled them. The panic remained, with no outlet save the galloping of her heart. Not even her voice could release a portion of her terror.

Nax!

The man released her and she fell through the hatch, stomach lifting. No ability to scream or twist or move her limbs to break her fall. But the impact she expected never came. Someone caught her.

The fall had unfolded the blanket. Air touched her bare skin.

"Put her there."

She was dropped onto the bed. The blanket tore away. She could do nothing. She was facing the wall. The men were behind her. A shadow stretched over her. A face loomed at the very furthest extent of her vision. She saw a hint of a white beard. "Kila Sigh, you have impressed me greatly."

"She isn't much," said the man who had caught her.

The ladder was straining under the weight of the man coming down from the attic.

Nax!

I'm here. Where are you?

In the barracks. The Donse Master has me. I can't move! I can't move. I have no—

The cat sent a bundle of emotion and sensation over the bond. Kila's panic retreated under the sensation of warmth and satiety. *We are trying to get to you, but there are too many men and hounds.*

"She doesn't look worth the effort," said one of the armsmen, as if he wanted the Donse Master to explain why they'd been troubled so greatly to find her. "Skinny as an atlen shank. What harm could she do anyone?"

"Great harm if she were to come into her power. One does not judge the mercusine by the bones of the merculyn."

Fight it! Nax sent.

How? He's using the mercus.

Fight.

A jingle of a purse being dumped out. "Here's my five gold, as promised," Skyll said.

"Thank you. I should fetch Radiant Hiolly. He ought to decide what to do with her, seeing as she's on his land."

"As an awakening merculyn she is the concern of the Way of Til. Radiant Hiolly will surely understand that. Bring her to my carriage." His hand brushed lightly over her cheek.

They did not cover her when they carried her out of the barracks. The night air bit with icy teeth, raising gooseflesh all over her body. She caught a glimpse of the Donse Master. He looked haggard in the glare of his own mercus light.

The other men had wandered back toward the barracks, having caught word that she'd been captured. A few servants came out to the kitchen garden to see her. They stared at her and invoked Til's name. One woman called her a harlot.

The carriage was built to carry four men. Two on one bench, two on the rear-facing bench. Kila was hoisted onto the latter. The carriage rocked and bounced as the Donse Master climbed aboard.

I'm in his carriage. Help me.

I know. You must fight it.

Nax felt very close. Kila thought she must be within arm's reach. But that was impossible.

The atlen team squawked under the driver's whip. The carriage began to roll.

"I'm curious, Sigh. Where did you stash PiTorro's blade?" He sat across from her, wand in one hand. There was a wooden box at his feet. The type of crate one might store potatoes in. There was a small brass object inside, glowing in her mercus vision.

Kila found her lips and tongue had been loosened from the spell. "What blade?"

Dunne Skyll chuckled.

Fight! Nax commanded.

Where are Fallo and Henley? The Donse Master is alone. They could overpower him. He's old and weak.

There are too many armsmen around the carriage.

Kila had forgotten that Dunne Skyll had come with his own contingent of armsmen. They must have been waiting outside the gate all this time. Which meant they were flanking the carriage on horseback even now. She listened for the clomp of hooves and heard them clearly. Her senses brought her their odor too. And a cat's.

Are you in this carriage?

Beneath it. Now fight. With the sending came another flood of emotion and sensation. It contained none of the comforting sensations from before. This was a feeling of warm and limber legs, of tense shoulders, of a readiness to jump and sprint. Her fingers were already clawed from holding the blanket tightly around her. The blanket was gone, but her fingers were frozen just as they'd been. But now a tingle went through them. She felt an extension of fibers in her fingers, as if she were spreading out claws. The disconcerting awareness of a flicking tail made her vision swim.

But that odd phantom tail flick awakened a smoldering ferocity. She had done nothing to deserve this treatment. She may be a thief, but she was a person. To be stilled like this, to be hauled out helpless before all those men, to be plopped on this bench like an aged ham, and then to be mocked by this man—intolerable.

Yes! Fight!

In every Cheapsgate alley, and in every encounter with a mark, Kila had faced the brutality of such men. Of clenched fists and grappling in the dark. She knew what it was to strain against muscle and bone; she knew the thoughtless and desperate struggle of one animal against another. Sometimes it was to overpower and rob, sometimes it was to break a hold and flee. Survival came down to pure, animal ruthlessness. There was nothing evil in it, nothing personal about it. Cats didn't hate the mice they killed.

And what of the ferocity of mice? Kila had been the mouse more often than she wanted to admit. The feeling of claws extending grew. While no mouse had ever become a hound, a girl could sometimes become too much of an armful, too much of a wild clawing and biting thing to be handled. She could see her hands, they were in front of her. No claws sprouted from fingertips, but her fingers moved. And strength pulsed through bone and tendon.

"You still hold the mercus," Dunne Skyll said. "Don't you feel it? I cannot understand how you gather so much yet fail to manifest anything with it." He leaned forward, cupping his bearded chin in one hand. He tapped her nose with his little wand. "You'll kill yourself doing that. The mind isn't meant to hold so much. It has to be released." The notion seemed to worry him. He pursed his lips and tilted his head, as if studying a bug he'd never seen before. "The Hargothe would relieve you of that excess, make no mistake. What else he might do with you . . . One can only imagine."

He smiled, but it didn't reach his eyes. He abruptly straightened, as if struck by an idea. He scrounged in a satchel on the seat next to him. Kila's toes moved. Her fingers were entirely free. While he was looking in his satchel she strained to flex her shoulders.

She resumed her pose of immobility just as he looked up. He withdrew PiTorro's dagger from his satchel. "I must say, dumping it in the cistern was clever. But it is very shiny and the water very clear." He held the blade awkwardly, like a man who considered weaponry beneath him. "I'm sure Dunne Postin will be coming to Appell's Inn to collect it. He'd better bring a fat purse."

The man held his pale wand in one hand and the dagger in the other. His mercus light was bright in the small carriage. It gleamed against the gold. But the inherent mercusine glow from the blade outshone even that. "Kil take you," she muttered, through stiff lips. He'd had the blade all along. He'd been toying her.

Nax pulsed a frenzy of feeling through the bond. It fed her anger. She tasted blood and grew ravenous with predatory hunger. The wand's hold on her stretched, thinned, strained. Skyll brought the tip of the dagger down and pressed it lightly on her throat. "I've never experienced anyone fight the willshift so ably. I don't sense any feat of mercus in you. So it is your will alone. I've read that powerful merculyns can overcome willshift. Pray you can muster as much should the Hargothe penetrate your mind."

He lifted the wand, focused on it. Kila's skin thrilled as a haze of prickliness enveloped the man. She gasped, realizing she was feeling his mercus power building. He withdrew the dagger from her throat and shook the wand at her. The constraints tightened around her shoulders, her wrists.

Nax no longer spoke into her mind, but simply jolted ferocity into Kila's body. She felt squeezed between warring energies. The glow of the dagger wavered in front of her. She locked her attention onto it as she clamped her jaw and battled the unseeable force that sought to reclaim hold of her limbs.

"I tire of this," he said. He wedged the lid from the box with the dagger, then set the dagger aside. He reached into the box and pulled Oly out by the scruff. The cat was limp, head lolling, pink tongue peeping from his mouth.

Nax! He has Oly!

I know. You must fight.

Is he dead?

No! But he will be if you don't fight!

Skyll lay Oly across his lap and took the dagger back up. He adjusted his grip and brought the tip of the dagger to Oly's flank. "Ah, I see in your eyes that you value this creature's life. But I wonder why a girl like you would have a cat for a pet. Surely you would wish to collect the bounty."

The gold dagger sang. Not in her hearing, but in her mind. It was infused with its own power, the demaynic charms Fallo had told of. Kila knew nothing of such things. But she saw more than mere metal in it now. Fallo had called it a hardblade. And so it was. A minute latticework of light suffused the metal. And it was this that sprang into her mercus vision.

She thought she could almost smell it, burnt hair and smoke. But there was more than sensory notes in its song. There was emotion too. Determination, ruthlessness, and a quality she could only label as speed. It didn't matter what such things were called. In her mercus vision, all things were sensation of one sort or another. Even emotion. *Especially* emotion.

She discovered in herself echoes of the blade's demaynic magic. She didn't know how to form it, let alone release it. But she grasped for it nonetheless. In a stilled moment, in the span between heartbeats, a shudder waved through her, from groin to heart to mind.

She wrenched back control of her own body. Dunne Skyll recoiled, mouth dropping open. The rod flipped from from his fingers as if it had stung him. He hissed and shook his hand. Kila unfolded, ignoring the cold in her limbs, ignoring the stiffness of her joints. Her focus remained entirely on the blade.

Skyll flicked it at her with an effiminate swing of his wrist. A man of no training. Were he not a Donse Master he would have been an easy mark to rob on a middlenight street. She grabbed his wrist as she lunged. She jammed her forearm into his throat and pushed hard. He squawked and gibbered.

Nax's endless feed of ferocity charged through her. She snarled like a beast, bent to sink her teeth into his neck. She stopped herself at the last instant and recoiled. *Stop it!* she sent to Nax. *I'm free.*

Her mind cleared. Skyll was beating her back and shoulder with one fist and scrabbling to stab her with the other. Oly slipped from his lap and back into the box. Kila put more weight onto his throat. She wrested the blade free of his grip, reversed it, and shoved.

His shoulders went rigid, his eyes bulged. A tight sigh hissed from his gaping mouth. His eyes met hers, pained, but no longer full of panic.

Kila panted, concious of sweat dripping down her back. The inside of the carriage was too loud with her breathing. The atlens still pulled the conveyance downslope. Horses clopped all around. Kila jumped off the man and retreated to the other bench. The hard-blade shone dully in her hand. Blood dripped from it. A spreading stain marred the Donse Master's robes. He looked dumbly down at it, hands crimson.

I think I killed him, she sent.

Good. Be ready.

For what?

Fallo and Henley will stop the carriage. We must run.

Where are you? She tipped over the seat to peer underneath. Nax wasn't there.

I'm under. On a thing. Kila's vision blurred and then she was seeing the road pass beneath her. Nax was riding under the carriage, balanced on a strut or cross brace.

Stop. You're gonna make me heave.

Her own vision returned. *Where are the boys going to stop us?*

A pause. *Lop says just before the Trialti Arch.*

Kila parted the window curtain and looked out. The Baths of Ori were blurring by. The arch was close, just around this bend and down.

Skyll tilted over onto one shoulder. His eyes were open. Breath still came. Kila clenched her teeth, the predatory rage now caged inside her. She scrounged through the Donse Master's robes, found his purse. His satchel held nothing save some papers and a partial loaf of bread. She put the dagger in the satchel and rolled it up.

A shout from the driver. The atlens shrieked. Men barked orders to clear the road. The brake lever squealed against the iron bands of the carriage wheels. Kila was jolted back in her seat as the carriage slowed. Dunne Skyll tumbled foward onto her. She kicked him off, shivering at the touch of his body against hers.

Go! Nax sent.

Kila grabbed Oly and burst from the carriage. She barely registered the obstacle Fallo and Henley had put in the road. An overturned hay wain. Then she was through the arch. Nax loped next to her, and without losing stride, jumped aboard and clawed up to Kila's shoulder.

Men shouted and horse hooves dug into the street behind her, their metal shoes clacking like hammer blows. Kila sprinted, head down through Dunne Medow Plaza. The Harridan Gate echoed with her gasps and footsteps. A sharp turn into an alley, then up to the roofway. She fell flat onto the top of the Myton Theatre and hugged Nax close. The satchel fell away, and Oly's body slid into a puddle. His body jerked and his head snapped up. He let out a yowl.

He's hurt!

No, Nax sent. *He's angry.*

What did that Donse Master do to him?

I don't know. But he's angry at you.

Me? What did I do?

The answer did not come for a long time. So long that Kila thought Nax had forgotten the question.

Oly says he almost got eaten by dogs because of you. He says you are stupid, selfish, foolish, and smelly.

At the moment, Kila didn't think she could fault Oly's judgment. Even though she'd just saved his miserable hide. *But what did the Donse Master do to him? I thought he was dead.*

Nax didn't seem to have the words to answer. Finally, she said, *He was limp on purpose.*

Playing dead.

He wants you to take the bell off him.

She pursed her lips and considered making Oly keep it. But they needed to be quiet until the street cleared. She cut the ribbon and carefully set the bell aside. Oly stomped away and sat down to give himself a good licking.

Thank you, Naxie, she sent, letting the little gray's ears filter through her fingers. *You saved me.*

The boys soon joined her. Lop and Huff nosed at Oly then came to greet her and Nax. They all huddled together as the shouts continued down below. "Murder! Murder!"

Men charged up and down the street. It was dawn before they gave up their hunt. By the time Kila and the boys returned to the atlen barn it was full daylight. Wen was asleep. Oly took pains not to wake him as he snuggled close.

Kila set the satchel onto the floor. The dagger inside clanked softly.

"That better not be what I think it is," Fallo said, eyebrow dipping over his nose.

"It is. We need to take it back to the Hiolly estate as soon as night falls," she said. "There's a cistern behind the house. Good hiding spot for it until your father decides to pay." Then she flopped onto her bed of rags, gathered Nax in her arms, and fell asleep. She didn't even hear Fallo's curses, much less see him take the satchel and leave the barn.

Nor did she see Henley watching her, knit cap in his hands. Had she, she would have marked his tender brow, his worried lips, and his immense relief.

SUCH A DIM MIND

The acolytes dragged the wounded Donse Master into the crypt. His soiled robe had been stripped away, his wound bandaged but not healed. His skin was scraped raw from another scrubbing.

"Leave him," came the raspy voice from the bed. The acolytes dropped Skyll onto the floor and backed from the overly warm room.

"You have disappointed me, Dunne Skyll. Did I not warn you that your new home awaited? Did you misunderstand me?"

Skyll did not answer.

"Your lover is already in her own cell. She shrieks most frightfully, my acolytes tell me."

Skyll did not answer.

"Make a light and see what your failures have wrought."

Time pulsed onward in absolute silence, for the

crypt was shielded from noise by its very design. "Make light, Skyll."

The Donse Master groaned and got onto his knees. A spark of mercus light bloomed near the low ceiling. The eyeless seer turned his face away from the glare. Skyll's head wobbled as he took in the scene. There was Dorlina, dressed in her Tilsday gown, tied to a chair. Not to restrain her, for she was dead. The bindings were to keep her upright. Her hair was unkempt, the skirts of her gown stained. Her fingernails were ragged and bloody, as if she'd been digging at stone.

"She had no mercus spark," the Hargothe said. "Hardly diverting to explore such a dim mind, save what I learned about you, Skyll. A doting father. I would never have guessed, even from the memories I ripped from your mind. Ah, but do not fear. I will not part you from her."

The door opened and acolytes swept in. They gathered Dorlina and Skyll and removed them from the crypt. The Donse Master's screams began a while later, but by then he was far down the corridor and beyond the door to the cell blocks. The Harogthe did not hear them. So he did not mark the moment when Skyll was shoved into his bone-filled cell, nor the shrieks when his beloved daughter was thrown in after him.

The Hargothe wondered absently how many days would pass before he succumbed to his hunger.

"Til is great," he said. Then he quoted his favorite passage from the Theb: "The agony of the faithless is His delight."

The world was corrupt. Through the Hargothe, all would be cleansed.

He summoned an acolyte with a mind probe. The man came, bent close. "Bring me Highest Chilow. I have work for him. As long as Sigh remains free, none shall rest."

LIKE A SKEPTICAL EYE

"Where is it?" she demanded, hands on hips.

"Safe," Fallo said. He was leaning back, hands behind his head. He wore the most disgustingly self-satisfied expression Kila had ever seen. The look of a young man who thought he was smarter than everyone else.

"You are scoundrel of the basest sort!" She had not endured all that she had just to have Fallo lose the blade. Not when they were so close to success.

Wen was sitting up, pale but revived from a fresh dose of Finta's medicine. The coin purse she'd taken from Dunne Skyll had paid that debt, but left little to spare. They needed the dagger and they needed PiTorro to pay. Wen did not seem particularly upset. He was more focused on petting Oly than on the test of wills before him.

It was Henley who interceded. He was always calm and thoughtful, refusing to be provoked by

Fallo's humor or Kila's impatience. "It's back at the Hiolly's."

"Why didn't you say so? Wait. You did that during the day?"

"It wasn't hard," Fallo said. "You told us on the way back here that Radiant Hiolly knew it was on his property and that if he found it, he would never give it back to my father. We figured that as long as it was there, it was still recoverable. If my father ever agrees to pay our fee."

Kila did not like the sound of this at all. "You *gave* it to Hiolly?"

"No. We sent it to him. We aren't stupid. It's in a nice package sent up with a courier."

Radiant Hiolly would lock it in a vault somewhere, along with all his extra gold. "If you had waited a little, I could have put it in the cistern. Or in a tree. Or in the barracks attic."

"If we had waited, Postin would have tracked it here. We've already lost one place to bed down, I wouldn't want to lose this one. Free eggs, after all."

"He's right, Kila," Wen said. "They did well. *You* did well. Plans are well and good, but the execution is always full of surprises. If we merit the title of recovery agents, we will be able to recover the blade. Until then, perhaps we should rest, for there is pickpocketing to do. And soon."

They sat down and ate some boiled atlen egg, and lazed away the day in the musty loft. Kila slept. When she next awoke it was dark. Wen's eyes were open. He had that look again. His mind was deep in a new scheme.

Wen is worried, Nax sent. *He knows what happened in the carriage.*

She had killed a man. The truth of it was stark in her mind. She found her throat aching and her breath tight. Skyll had deserved it, but that fact didn't lift the burden. When she'd leapt across that carriage, she'd crossed a bridge. It went only one way, collapsing behind. From thief to killer. From taking coin to taking life.

As a Cheapsgater in Starside, life was steal or starve. Every attempt to claw out of her day-to-day, purse to mouth existence had met with failure. This hope that PiTorro would hire them seem suddenly foolish, childish. A notion so fanciful it was fit only for a storybook.

She got up and climbed from the barn. Nax followed as she went to the roofway. The night was cold, but the sky was clear. The moon stood over the city like a skeptical eye, half-lidded and wary. In the distance she thought she heard a raven cry.

She wasn't superstitious, but she shivered and tapped her ear three times. "Die, raven, die."

You are different, Nax said.

Kila stretched and breathed in the salty air. There would be drunken men on the street tonight. *What do you mean?*

When I found you, you were a scavenger.

And now?

There was no pause in the answer, but Nax's words

were preceeded by a flurry of images and sensations. Of crouching in the dark, of supremely keen vision watching movement below, of intense hunger burning in her belly. These feelings stopped and Nax sent with great approval, *Now you are a predator.*

~

The End of *Thief of Sparks*, book one of Starside Saga. The epic continues in *A Raven's Dream.*

Sign up for my newsletter to get the **free** Starside short story, *Caverns of Misen-Tine*, an exclusive gift to newsletter subscribers. *Caverns* is the amazing "origin story" of Fallo.

Get it at ericedstrom.com / free-starside-story

Keep reading more of Starside Saga

Kila Sigh's adventures continue in *A Raven's Dream, Mind of Mercusine, The Raven Throne, The Force of Destiny, The Shadline Rises, Fortress of Shadow, Dagger of Deception.* All are full novels, and all are out now!

As her magic powers grow, Kila draws the attention of powerful allies and even more powerful enemies.

In the ancient city of Starside, the mysterious seer known as The Hargothe has felt Kila Sigh awaken to her magical powers. He desires nothing more than to possess both her and her bonded telepathic cat Nax.

But other forces have felt her, too. Some hoping to protect her, some wanting to kill her. As Kila and her family of thieves and cats search for the missing Finta Sahng—the only person who makes the medicine Kila's brother needs—they stumble on an city beneath the city. When Kila faces the loss of everything she cares for, she must dig deep for the power to destroy all who stand against her.

Visit ericedstrom.com for a complete list of Eric's fantastic fiction.

9 781947 518124